"Stay the night, Portia, and drive back in the morning."

So Jean-Christophe Lucien Brissac was no different from the rest after all. Portia removed her hand, utterly astounded by the discovery that she was deeply tempted to say yes.

"No, I can't do that," she said quietly. "I'm accustomed to long journeys in any weather."

"I was not asking to share your room, Miss Grant," Luc said icily. "My concern was for your safety only. You mistake me. Also you insult me."

She frowned. "Insult you?"

"Yes. It is not my habit to force my way into a woman's bed. Even a woman as alluring and challenging as you," he informed her.

D1021193

CATHERINE GEORGE was born in Wales, and early on developed a passion for reading, which eventually fueled her compulsion to write. Marriage to an engineer led to nine years in Brazil, but on his later travels the education of her son and daughter kept her in the U.K. And instead of constant reading to pass her lonely evenings she began to write the first of her romantic novels. When not writing and reading she loves to cook, listen to opera and browse in antiques shops.

Books by Catherine George

HARLEQUIN PRESENTS®
2059—AN ENGAGEMENT OF CONVENIENCE

Don't miss any of our special offers. Write to us at the
following address for information on our newest releases.

Harlequin Reader Service
U.S.: 3010 Walden Ave., P.O. Box 1325, Buffalo, NY 14269
Canadian: P.O. Box 609, Fort Erie, Ont. L2A 5X3

Catherine George

LUC'S REVENGE

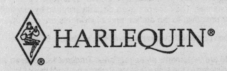

HARLEQUIN®

TORONTO • NEW YORK • LONDON
AMSTERDAM • PARIS • SYDNEY • HAMBURG
STOCKHOLM • ATHENS • TOKYO • MILAN • MADRID
PRAGUE • WARSAW • BUDAPEST • AUCKLAND

If you purchased this book without a cover you should be aware
that this book is stolen property. It was reported as "unsold and
destroyed" to the publisher, and neither the author nor the
publisher has received any payment for this "stripped book."

ISBN 0-373-12113-X

LUC'S REVENGE

First North American Publication .

Copyright © by Catherine George.

All rights reserved. Except for use in any review, the reproduction or
utilization of this work in whole or in part in any form by any electronic,
mechanical or other means, now known or hereafter invented, including
xerography, photocopying and recording, or in any information storage
or retrieval system, is forbidden without the written permission of the
publisher, Harlequin Enterprises Limited, 225 Duncan Mill Road,
Don Mills, Ontario, Canada M3B 3K9.

All characters in this book have no existence outside the imagination of
the author and have no relation whatsoever to anyone bearing the same
name or names. They are not even distantly inspired by any individual
known or unknown to the author, and all incidents are pure invention.

This edition published by arrangement with Harlequin Books S.A.

® and TM are trademarks of the publisher. Trademarks indicated with
® are registered in the United States Patent and Trademark Office, the
Canadian Trade Marks Office and in other countries.

Visit us at www.eHarlequin.com

Printed in U.S.A.

CHAPTER ONE

THE call came late on a Friday evening, when everyone else had left for the weekend. On the way out herself when the phone rang, Portia was tempted to leave the call to the answering service. But with an impatient sigh she turned back at last and picked up the receiver.

'Whitefriars Estates. Good evening.'

'Good evening. I am flying in from Paris tomorrow to see one of your properties. Your name, please?'

The voice was male, French and imperious.

'Miss Grant,' said Portia crisply. 'If you'll just give me the details.'

'First please understand that the appointment must be tomorrow evening. At five. I arranged this with your Mr Parrish.'

Portia stiffened. 'That's very short notice, Monsieur—'

'Brissac. But it is not short notice. Mr Parrish informed me last week that one of the partners at your agency was always on hand at weekends for viewings. He said it was merely a matter of confirmation. You *are* a partner?' he added, with a pejorative note of doubt.

'Yes, Monsieur Brissac, I am.' Portia's eyes narrowed ominously. Ben Parrish, one of the senior partners, had just left for a skiing weekend in Gstaad without a word about this peremptory Frenchman. 'Perhaps you would tell me which property you have in mind and I'll do my best to make the arrangements.'

'I wish to inspect Turret House,' he informed her, and Portia stood rooted to the spot.

The property was not in London, as expected, but a three-hour drive away on the coast. But, more ominous than that, it was a house she'd hoped never to set foot in again as long as she lived. During the lengthy time it had been on their books Ben Parrish had always taken prospective buyers over Turret House. Not that there had ever been many. And none at all lately. The property was sticking. But personal feelings couldn't be allowed to lose a sale.

'Are you still there, *mademoiselle*?'

'Yes, Monsieur Brissac. This is very short notice, but I'll arrange my diary to fit the visit in.'

'You will come yourself, of course.'

Portia's eyes glittered coldly. 'Of course. My assistant will accompany me.' She saw no reason to tell him that Biddy was at home, nursing a cold.

'As you wish. I shall not, you understand, expect you to drive back to London afterwards,' he informed her. 'The Ravenswood Hotel is nearby. There is a double room reserved for you in the name of Whitefriars Estates. Please make use of it.'

'That won't be necessary,' she said at once.

'*Au contraire*. I shall require a return visit to Turret House very early the following morning.'

'I'm afraid that's not possible.'

'But this was the arrangement made with Mr Parrish, *mademoiselle*. It was made clear that someone would be available to escort me round the property.'

Ben Parrish might be one of her senior partners, but she would have a bone to pick with him when he came back from the *piste*. 'As I said, I'll cancel my private arrangements and meet you at Turret House, Monsieur

Brissac,' Portia assured him. 'But a hotel room is unnecessary. I'm used to driving long distances.'

'In this case it would be unwise. You must be available very early on Sunday. I return to Paris later in the morning.'

Heaping vengeance on the absent Ben's head, Portia had no option but to agree. 'As you wish, Monsieur Brissac.'

'Thank you, *mademoiselle*. Your name again, please?'

'Grant.'

'*A demain*, Miss Grant.'

Until tomorrow. Which threatened to be very different from her original plans for Saturday. Her eyes stormy, Portia put the phone down, checked that Whitefriars Estates was secure for the night, and went home.

Home was a flat in a building in Chiswick, with a fantastic view of the Thames and an equally fantastic mortgage. The apartment was a recent acquisition, with big rooms only sparsely furnished as yet. But the view was panoramic and the building secure, and Portia loved it. All her life she'd lived with other people in one way or another. But the moment she'd moved into the empty flat Portia had experienced such an exhilarating sense of liberation she never begrudged a minute of the years of hard work, both past and future, which made her pricey retreat possible.

Despite her protests to the peremptory Monsieur Brissac, Portia had no private appointments to cancel. Her plan had been to rent some videos, send out for her favourite food, and do absolutely nothing the entire weekend. And do it alone. Something her male colleagues at the firm viewed as eccentric in the extreme.

'A woman like you,' Ben Parrish had informed her
once, 'should be lighting up some lucky bloke's life.'

An opinion Portia viewed as typically male. She liked
her life the way it was, and the social side of it was busy
enough, normally. But, as Ben Parrish had known very
well, it was her turn to keep the weekend free, in case
some well-heeled client should suddenly demand a viewing of one of the expensive properties handled by
Whitefriars Estates. Her only cause for complaint was
the fact that Turret House was the property in question
this weekend.

'You're unnatural,' her friend Marianne had com-
plained once. She was on the editorial staff of a glossy
magazine, rushed from one hectic love affair to another,
and came flying to Portia for consolation between bouts.
'All you care about is that job, and this place. You might
as well buy a cat and settle into total spinsterhood.'

Portia had been unmoved. 'I don't like cats. And the
term "spinster", Ms Taylor, is no longer politically cor-
rect.'

'Nor does it apply to you, darling, yet. But it might
if you don't watch out!'

Portia drove home, had a bath, put some supper together, then opened her briefcase and with reluctance
settled down to study the brochure of Turret House. The
recent owners had renovated it throughout, but she was
surprised the Frenchman was interested in it. Turret
House was in immaculate condition now, according to
Ben Parrish, but it was big, expensive, in a remote location, and not even pleasing to the eye unless one had
a taste for the Gothic. Built as a dower house for the
owner of Ravenswood, the architecture was typical of
the latter part of Victoria's reign. These days
Ravenswood was an expensive country house hotel, and

Turret House a separate property far too big to attract the average family. Portia eyed the brochure with foreboding. Tomorrow would be a deeply personal ordeal, but otherwise a complete waste of time. The man would take one look at the house, give a Gallic shudder of distaste, and race back to Paris on the next plane. She brightened. In which case she could shake off the dust of Turret House for ever, drive back to London and take up her weekend where she'd left off.

The February afternoon was bright with cold sunshine as Portia drove west next day along the crowded motorway. She made good time, eventually turned off into the West Country, and arrived well on schedule at the crossroads between Ravenswood and Turret House. Her reluctance deepened as she took the familiar right-hand fork to head for the house she'd hoped never to set eyes on again. But as she slowed to turn into the drive Portia sternly controlled her misgivings. She took professional note of the refurbished splendour of the gates and the well-tended air of the tiered garden as she negotiated the hairpin bends of the steep drive. At last, no matter how slowly she drove, she reached the gravelled terrace and came face to face with Turret House again.

Portia switched off the ignition, but remained in the car for a while. With time to spare before her client arrived, she put her feelings aside and tried to view the house with a purchaser's eye as the last rays of sunset light glittered on arched windows and flamed on red brick walls. It was a typical, rambling villa of its era, with a turreted square tower stuck on the end like an afterthought—the taste of the self-made industrialist who'd bought elegant, Palladian Ravenswood for his aristocratic bride. And promptly built Turret House three miles away for his mother-in-law.

Unable to put off the moment any longer, Portia got out of the car, shivering more with apprehension than cold. She belted her long winter white coat tightly, pulled her velvet Cossack hat low over her eyes, collected her briefcase and crossed the terrace to the arched front door. She breathed in deeply, then unlocked the door, switched on the lights, and stood still in surprise on the threshold. She had noted the renovations in the brochure, but it was still strange to find the old red Turkey carpet gone and the austere beauty of the black and white tiles left bare. And the heavy dark wood of the staircase had been stripped and sealed, the artistry of the carving revealed now by the light from the stained-glass window on the landing. Portia let out the breath she'd been holding. The hall was so much smaller than her memory of it. But, most important of all, it was empty. No ghosts at all.

Almost light-headed with relief, Portia went through the rest of the rooms, switching on lights, noting the quality of the pale carpets and the padded silk curtains. No furniture, which was a drawback. It was much easier to sell an inhabited, furnished house. Which was probably why the place was sticking. And upstairs everything was so unfamiliar it could have been a different house. Smaller rooms had been converted into bathrooms to connect with the larger bedrooms, and the pastel paint everywhere was a far cry from the dark gloom of the past. Portia glanced at her watch, frowning, then went back downstairs. The client was an hour late. And Turret House was not a place she cared to linger in after dark.

Nor, Portia found, could she bring herself to look over the tower rooms alone first. A cold shiver ran through her at the mere thought. She turned on her heel and went back to the bright, welcoming kitchen instead, hoping

Monsieur Brissac was bringing the woman in his life.
Kitchens were a very important selling point. These days
very few clients wanted a formal dining room as the only
place to eat. Fortunately the vendors had joined the old
larder to the kitchen to form one vast room, with space
for an eating area. In contrast to the old-fashioned, com-
fortless place of the past, the result was a glossy magazine vision of a country kitchen, complete with fashionable dark blue Aga stove.

Portia stood very still, staring at it. There had been an
Aga stove in the past, coal-fired and ancient, its beige
enamel discoloured with age and constant use. It had
been a devil to load and rake out...

A voice outside in the hall plucked Portia back into
the present. She went through the leather-backed door to
find a tall man craning his neck to look up the staircase,
impatience radiating from him like nuclear fallout.

Portia coughed. 'Monsieur Brissac?'

He swung round sharply, the impatience falling from
him like a cloak as she moved forward under the bare
central light of the hall. He bowed slightly, his eyes nar-
rowing as he saw her face. '*Pardon.* The door was open
so I came in. My plane was delayed. If I kept you waiting I am sorry.'

Even at first glance Portia doubted that penitence was
part of this man's make-up. 'How do you do?' she said
politely.

He was silent for a moment, taking in every detail of
her appearance. 'You are Miss Grant from Whitefriars
Estates?'

'Yes. Unfortunately my assistant's ill and couldn't
come,' she admitted reluctantly, and returned his scrutiny with interest. He wore a formal dark overcoat, worn
open over a city suit, and he was younger than she'd

expected, with thick, longish black hair and smooth olive skin, a straight noise. But his mouth curved in strikingly sensuous contrast to the firm, dark-shadowed jaw. And something about him revived the feeling of unease she'd experienced at the first sound of his voice on the phone.

'I had expected someone older, *mademoiselle*,' he said at last.

So had Portia. But you're stuck with me, she thought silently, then stiffened as a sudden gleam in his eyes told her he'd read her mind. Reminding herself that her mission was to sell the house, not alienate the client, she exerted herself to please as she took him on a tour of the ground-floor rooms, extolling virtues of space and the wonderful views by daylight over the bay.

'A pity you arrived so late,' she said pleasantly. 'The view is a major attraction of Turret House.'

'So I was told.' He raised a quizzical eyebrow. 'Is it good enough to compensate for the architecture? You must admit that the exterior lacks charm.'

'True. But the house was built to last.' Portia led the way upstairs, pointing out the various selling points as her elegant client explored the bedrooms. On the way downstairs again she stressed the advantages of the immaculate interior decoration, the new central heating system, the recent rewiring, the curtains and carpets included in the price. In the kitchen, she pointed out its practical and aesthetic virtues, but at last there was only the tower left to explore. Portia preceded her client into the hall, her pulse racing and her hands clammy as she pressed a button in the wall beneath the stairwell. A door slid aside in the panelling to reveal a lift. 'This is set in the turret itself,' she said colourlessly. 'It takes you to the bedroom floor, of course, then on to the top room in the tower, Monsieur Brissac.'

He smiled. 'Ah! You saved the *pièce de résistance* for last, Miss Grant. Is it in good working order?'

'Yes,' she said, devoutly hoping she was right. 'To demonstrate this we can inspect the three floors of the tower on foot, then call the lift up to the top floor to bring us down again.'

Wishing now she'd forced herself to inspect the tower alone first, Portia preceded her client into the ground-floor room, a light, airy apartment, with windows on the three outer walls. And empty, just like the hall. She relaxed slightly. 'I believe this was used as the morning room by the lady of the house when it was first built. This door opens into the lift, and the one beside it conceals a spiral stair to the next floor.' Straight-backed, Portia led the way up the winding stair to a room similar to the one below, then, at last, her heart beating like a war drum, she ran quickly up the last flight to the top of the tower. She switched on the light, waved her client ahead of her into the room, then stood just inside the door, her back against the wall, feeling giddy with relief.

'The view here is quite marvellous in the daytime,' she said breathlessly.

The Frenchman eyed her with concern. 'You are very pale. Are you unwell, *mademoiselle*?'

'No. I'm fine.' She managed a smile. 'Out of condition. I need more exercise.'

He looked unconvinced. 'But not at this moment, I think. Is this the button for the *ascenseur*? Let us test its efficiency.'

In the claustrophobic, strangely threatening confines of the small elevator Portia felt hemmed in by her companion's physical proximity, very conscious of dark, narrowed eyes fixed on her face as they glided silently to the ground floor.

'Most impressive,' he remarked as they went out into the hall.

'Installed in the early part of the century, when the house was fitted with electricity,' said Portia unevenly, the blood beginning to flow normally in her veins once they were out of the tower. 'Have you seen everything you want, Monsieur Brissac?'

'For the moment, yes. Tomorrow, in daylight, I shall make a more detailed inspection. I believe there is a path down to a private cove?'

Portia nodded. 'But there's been no maintenance work done on it for a long time. I'm not sure how safe it is.'

'If the weather permits we shall explore and find out.' He frowned slightly. 'You have not shown other prospective purchasers round Turret House?'

'Oh, yes. Quite a number,' she contradicted him quickly. 'The property's attracted a lot of interest.'

'I meant you, personally, Miss Grant.'

'Myself, no, I haven't,' she admitted. 'My colleague, Mr Parrish, owns a weekend cottage in the area, so he usually does the viewing.' She smiled politely. 'Have you any more questions?'

'Of course, many more. But I shall ask them tomorrow.' He glanced at his watch. 'Soon it will be time for our dinner. Let us drive to the hotel.'

Our dinner?

Again he read her mind with ease. He smiled. 'I am entertaining some clients to dinner at the Ravenswood. Will you join us?'

Portia shook her head. 'You're very kind, but I won't, thanks. It's an early start tomorrow, so I'll have supper in my room, then get some sleep.'

'A boring programme,' he observed as Portia switched off the last of the lights.

'But very attractive to me after a busy working week,' she assured him pleasantly.

'Then I trust you will enjoy it. *Alors*, you will go first so I can make sure you arrive at Ravenswood safely.'

With no intention of telling him she knew the area like the back of her hand, Portia said goodbye, got in her car, and drove swiftly down the winding drive, then accelerated into the narrow road, intent on getting to the hotel before him. But by the time she'd parked under the trees in the courtyard and taken her overnight bag from her boot her client was at her elbow, to take the bag and escort her into the foyer.

'This is Miss Grant of Whitefriars Estates,' he informed the pretty receptionist. The girl greeted him warmly, consulted a computer screen and handed Portia a key.

'Twenty-four?' he said, frowning. 'Is that the best you can do, Frances? What other rooms are free tonight?'

'None, I'm afraid, Monsieur Brissac.' She eyed him uncertainly. 'Some of the guests haven't arrived yet. Shall I juggle a bit?'

He shook his head. 'No, *I* shall take twenty-four. Give Miss Grant my room. She appreciates a view.'

The obliging Frances dimpled. 'All the rooms have views, Monsieur Brissac.'

'But some are more beautiful than others,' he countered, smiling. Frances flushed and handed over a new key to her guest, something in her eyes which rather puzzled Portia. It was only later, in the large, inviting room with a tester bed and a view over floodlit parkland, that she realised the receptionist had felt envious. And, much against her will, she could understand why. Monsieur Brissac was a formidably attractive man, with a charm she was by no means wholly immune to herself.

But the charm was oddly familiar. Yet she was quite
certain she'd never met him before. Her client wasn't
the type of man women forgot.

Portia unpacked her overnight bag deep in thought.
The dimpled Frances obviously knew this Brissac man
very well. Was he the hotel manager? That didn't fit,
somehow, if he was inspecting a nearby property. Maybe
he was just a customer, regular and valued enough to
ask a favour. In which case, what, exactly, *was* the favour? Maybe his room was next door, and this was the
reason for the envy. Portia made a swift inspection, but
there was no connecting door to another room. She
frowned, annoyed with herself. Going back to Turret
House again had addled her brain. Monsieur Brissac's
impatience had quickly changed to something different—and familiar—the moment he'd taken a good look
at her, it was true. But otherwise he'd been faultlessly
circumspect. He'd tuned in sharply enough to her un-
easiness in Turret House, though. Which was unsurpris-
ing. Her reluctance had been hard to hide as they entered
the tower, and her relief equally obvious when they left
it. Tomorrow she would be more in control, now the
initial ordeal was over.

Portia had packed very little. With no intention of
eating in the dining room, a suitable dress had been unnecessary. A couple of novels and some room service
completed her plan for an evening spent in remarkably
pleasant surroundings. The room was quite wonderful,
with luxuriously comfortable chairs and sofa, and gleaming bronze lamps. On a low table magazines flanked a
silver tray laden with glasses, a decanter of sherry, dishes
of nuts and tiny savoury biscuits. And a refrigerator mas-
querading as an antique chest held soft drinks and various spirits and wines, even champagne.

Portia took a quick look at the menus on the dressing table, then rang for tea to tide her over until the lobster salad she'd chosen for dinner later on. Once the tea tray arrived Portia tipped the polite young waiter and locked the door behind him. She pulled off her hat, unpinned her hair and ran her fingers through crackling bronze curls which sprang free as though glad to escape. Then she removed her tailored brown suit and silk shirt and hung them up, pulled off her long suede boots and removed her stockings, then wrapped herself in the white towelling dressing gown provided by the hotel. With a sigh of pleasure she sank down on the sofa with a cup of tea, nibbled on one of the accompanying petits fours, and gazed out over parkland lit so cleverly it looked bathed with moonlight.

When she was young it had always been her ambition to stay in the Ravenswood, which featured in smart magazines, offering weekend breaks of unbridled luxury. The room was exquisitely furnished, and the bathroom was vast, with a tub big enough to swim in and everything else a guest could need, right down to a separate telephone. A bit different from her usual company-funded overnight stops when inspections or viewings took her too far to return to base overnight.

So now, surprisingly, she could resume her plans for the weekend right here. She could read, watch a television programme, even request a video from the list provided.

Portia got up to draw the curtains, then picked up her book and prepared to enjoy the evening just as she'd planned to at home. Only tonight, after a long, leisurely bath, she would read herself to sleep in the picturesque tester bed, and someone would bring her breakfast on a tray in the morning. Wonderful. When a knock heralded the arrival of her dinner, punctual to the minute, Portia tightened the sash on the dressing gown and went on bare feet to open the door to the waiter. And confronted the elegant figure of Monsieur Brissac instead.

They stared at each other for a moment in mutual surprise, then his eyes moved from her bare feet to the tumbled hair. She thrust it back quickly, heat rising in her face as her pulse astonished her by racing at the sight of him. The Frenchman was obviously fresh from a shower, the dark shadow along his jaw less evident, and he was wearing a different, equally elegant suit. 'Is your room to your taste, Miss Grant?' he enquired, moving closer.

Portia backed away instinctively. 'Yes, indeed. Very comfortable. But I'm expecting my dinner to arrive any moment, so if you'll excuse me—'

'My guests tell me they are suffering from jet lag and wish to retire early,' he interrupted smoothly. 'Since you will not dine with us, perhaps you would join me in the bar later this evening, Miss Grant. I wish to discuss certain aspects of the sale of Turret House before we return to it in the morning.'

Refusing to let the intent dark eyes fluster her, Portia thought swiftly. Her partners were about to suggest a price reduction to the owners. If she could make the sale at the present price it would be a feather in her cap. As junior partner, and a female, she was secretly driven by the need to compete on equal terms with the men at Whitefriars.

'After dinner, in the bar?' he prompted, obviously amused by her hesitation.

Portia nodded briskly. 'Of course, if you feel further discussion will be useful before seeing the house again. Perhaps you'll ring me when you're free.' No way was she hanging about in the bar until he was ready to join her.

'Of course, Miss Grant.' He smiled. 'Enjoy your dinner.'

Portia returned the smile and closed the door, then stood against it for a moment, giving herself a stringent little lecture as she waited for her pulse-rate to return to normal. Charm personified he might be, but Monsieur Brissac was just a client. And she was here solely to sell him a house.

When her lobster salad arrived Portia eyed it in surprise. Not only was it a work of art on a plate, but it was accompanied by a half-bottle of Premier Cru burgundy, a small mound of gleaming black caviare as appetiser, and an iced parfait of some kind to round off the feast.

'No mistake, Miss Grant,' said the receptionist when Portia rang to enquire. 'Compliments of Monsieur Brissac.'

Portia thanked the girl, shrugged, then began to spread caviare on crisp squares of toast, wondering why she was being entertained so lavishly. It was she who wanted Monsieur Brissac's business, not the other way round. What was his motive? On the phone he'd been demanding almost to the point of rudeness, but in person, once he'd actually met her, deliberate charm had quickly replaced his initial impatience. Yet something about him made her uneasy. Unable to pinpoint the reason for it, Portia despatched the last of the caviare, then helped herself to some mayonnaise from a small porcelain pot and began on the lobster she could rarely afford. Tonight it had been a reward to herself for her disturbing day. She had assumed she would pay for it herself, but Monsieur Brissac had taken pains to show he was footing the bill. Yet if Ben Parrish had been in charge of the viewing he would have expected to pay for both his own dinner and the client's to oil the wheels of the transaction.

But she was an attractive woman, so the situation was different. Portia had no illusions about her looks. An accident of nature had given her a face, hair and a shape most of her women friends envied. Because she'd been wearing a hat, and a long coat which covered her from throat to ankle, Mr Brissac would have had to guess about shape and hair. But his impatience had evaporated the moment he'd taken a good look at her face at Turret House. And a few minutes ago his eyes had gleamed with something else entirely at the sight of her in a robe, with her hair all over the place.

Portia frowned thoughtfully. Monsieur Brissac, she was sure, was too sophisticated and subtle a man to try to mix business with pleasure. Tonight he had taken her by surprise. But from now on she would be in control, totally poised and professional. And in the meantime nothing was going to spoil her pleasure in her dinner.

CHAPTER TWO

WHEN the telephone rang just after ten Portia decided on a little dressage. Monsieur Brissac might whistle, but she wasn't coming running just yet.

'Would you give me another fifteen minutes or so?' she asked pleasantly.

'But of course. As long as you wish,' he assured her.

Portia had taken time over a bath and washing her hair. Sorry now she'd been so frugal with her packing, her sole concession to the occasion was a fresh silk T-shirt with the suit worn earlier—her usual office clothes. She brushed her newly washed hair up into as tight a knot as possible and pinned it securely, replaced the amber studs in her earlobes, then collected handbag and key and went off to charm Monsieur Brissac into buying Turret House.

The bar was crowded with well-dressed people in convivial mood after the pleasures of the impressive Ravenswood dinner menu. When Portia paused in the doorway the elegant figure of her client rose to his feet at a small table in a far corner.

'I'm sorry if I've kept you waiting,' she said politely, as he held a chair for her.

'You did not,' he assured her, smiling. 'You are punctual to the second. May I offer you a cognac with your coffee?'

No way, thought Portia. She needed to keep her faculties needle-sharp since her companion was making it clear that though they were here to discuss business he was taking unconcealed male pleasure in her company.

'I won't, thank you.' She smiled at him. 'Just coffee.'

Even before she'd finished speaking a waitress had materialised with a tray and put it on the low table in front of her.

Monsieur Brissac smiled his thanks at the girl, then filled their cups and handed one to Portia. She added a dash of cream, refused one of the handmade chocolates he offered, then sat back, waiting for questions.

Instead he looked at her in silence, examining her face feature by feature in a way Portia found unsettling. 'So, Monsieur Brissac,' she began briskly. 'What can I tell you about Turret House?'

He leaned forward and added sugar to his cup, and almost absently Portia noted his slim, strong hands, the small gold signet ring on his little finger, the fine dark hair visible on the wrist below a gleaming white shirt-cuff fastened with a gold cufflink of the same design as the ring.

'First of all, tell me why the owners wish to sell,' he said. 'Is there some drawback to the house not immediately apparent?'

'No,' she assured him. 'Make any survey you want, but I guarantee you'll find the house is sound, and the wiring and plumbing in perfect order. The roof has been renewed, and unless it's a matter of conflicting taste, neither exterior nor interior need repair or redecoration.'

'Then why should the owners want to sell a house they took so much care to renovate and modernise?'

Portia smiled ruefully. 'Unfortunately a very common reason. Divorce.'

'Ah. I see.' He nodded. 'A pity. Turret House is meant for a large family.'

'Is that why you're interested in it?'

'No. I am not married.' He gave a characteristically Gallic shrug. 'At least not yet. And, since you are *Miss* Grant, I assume you are not married either.'

'No, I'm not.' She changed the subject. 'So, what else would you like to know?'

'Your first name,' he said, surprising her.

'Portia,' she said, after a pause.

He glanced down into his cup quickly, giving Portia a view of enviable dark lashes. 'So. Your parents were fond of your William Shakespeare.' He looked up again, his eyes holding hers. 'And do you possess the quality of mercy, Mademoiselle Portia?'

Portia willed her pulse to behave itself. 'My name is nothing to do with Shakespeare, Monsieur Brissac. My father was a car enthusiast.'

He frowned. *'Comment?'*

'He loved fast cars, the Porsche most of all. So I'm named after it. But my mother held out for Shakespeare's spelling.'

He gave a husky, delighted laugh. 'Your father had vision,' he told her.

'In what way?'

'The Porsche is small, elegant and very efficient. The description fits you perfectly. I like your name very much,' he said. 'Will you allow me to use it?'

If he bought Turret House he could call her what he liked. 'Of course, if you wish.'

'Then you must respond.' He half rose with a little bow, then reseated himself. 'Allow me to introduce myself. Jean-Christophe Lucien Brissac.'

Her eyebrows rose. 'A lot of names.''

''I am known as Luc,' he informed her.

She shook her head. 'It's not my practice to be on first-name terms with clients.'

'But in this case, if I purchase Turret House, you will have a great deal to do with me in future, Portia,' he pointed out.

She pounced. 'And are you going to buy it, then?'

'I might. Tomorrow, if my second impression is as good as the first, and if we can negotiate the price a little, there is a strong possibility that you and I may do business, Portia.'

She kept iron control on every nerve to hide her excitement. 'That sounds very encouraging.'

'But there is another condition to the sale,' he informed her.

Portia stiffened. 'Condition?'

'You must tell me the truth. Does Turret House possess a *revenant*? Is there a ghost, Portia?' His eyes held hers so steadily she discovered they were of a shade of green so dark that to the casual eye it was hard to distinguish iris from pupil.

'Not to my knowledge,' she said without inflection. 'The house isn't nearly as old as this one, remember. Ghosts are more likely at Ravenswood than Turret House.'

'Yet for a moment, at the top of that extraordinary tower, I thought you were going to faint,' he went on relentlessly. 'And do not tell me you were breathless or unfit. Your tension was tangible.'

Portia looked away, fighting down the formless, unidentifiable fear she experienced at the mere mention of the tower. Poised and professional, she reminded herself, and turned to look at him very directly. 'Monsieur Brissac—'

'Luc.'

'Very well, Luc. If you buy the property I guarantee that neither you, nor anyone who lives there, will be troubled by ghosts. Turret House is not haunted.'

Straight dark brows drew together as Luc Brissac tapped a slim finger against the bottom lip which struck Portia anew as arrestingly sensuous above the firmly clenched jaw.

'Alors,' he said slowly, his eyes intent on hers. 'If I decide to buy, will you tell me what troubled *you* there today?'

'Is that a condition of sale?'

'No. But I am—interested. I could sense your distress. It disturbed me very much.'

Portia gazed at him, rather shaken. 'All right. If you decide to buy, I'll tell you.'

Luc Brissac reached out a hand to shake hers gravely. 'A deal, Miss Portia.'

'A deal,' she agreed, and looked down at their clasped hands, not liking to pull hers away, but very much aware that his fingers were on the pulse reacting so traitorously to his touch.

'Goodnight, Portia,' he said, very quietly, and raised her hand to his lips before releasing it.

She rose rather precipitately. 'If that's everything for the moment, it's time for that early night I promised myself.'

He walked with her through the now almost empty bar. 'Sleep well.'

'I'm sure I shall. It's a beautiful room.' She hesitated, then looked up at him very squarely. 'Thank you for turning it over to me. And for the dinner. It wasn't necessary for you to provide it, but I enjoyed it very much.'

Luc Brissac frowned. 'But I told you I had reserved

a room, Portia. Naturally I would provide dinner and breakfast also.''

'If I was anxious for you to clinch the deal shouldn't I have been buying *you* dinner?' She paused at the foot of the wide, shallow staircase.

He smiled. 'Perhaps when I return to London to finalise matters you might still do that?'

Portia's heart leapt beneath the silk shirt. 'Of course,' she said quickly. 'The firm will be happy to entertain you.'

'I meant *you*, Portia.' His smile faded. 'Or is the deal the price I must pay for more of your company?'

'In the circumstances I can't think of a reply which wouldn't offend you.' She smiled to soften the words. 'And I try to avoid offending clients, so I'll say goodnight.'

He returned the smile and bowed slightly. 'Be ready at eight in the morning, Portia. Your breakfast will arrive at seven-thirty.'

Portia woke early next day, with more than enough time to shower and dress and pack her belongings before breakfast. According to Ben Parrish, other clients had declined a scramble down to the cove. But something about Luc Brissac's voice had warned her that this particular client would be different, so she'd come prepared, with a heavy cream wool sweater, brown wool trousers and flat leather shoes in her luggage. And an amber fleece jacket instead of her pale winter coat. When she was ready she enjoyed the freshly squeezed orange juice and feathery, insubstantial croissants, and went downstairs at the appointed hour, her overnight bag in one hand, her coat slung over the other arm. And experienced the now familiar leap in her blood at the sight of Luc Brissac.

'Such British punctuality,' he said, coming to meet her. '*Bonjour*, Portia. You slept well?'

'Good morning. I slept very well indeed,' she returned, with absolute truth. Which was a surprise, one way and another.

Conscious of discreet interest from the reception desk, Portia surrendered her bag to Luc, who was informal this morning in a rollneck sweater and serviceable cords.

When they went out into a cold, bright morning, Portia was thankful to see the day was fine. Turret House would make a better second impression in sunlight.

Luc stowed the bag in her car, then informed her he would drive her in his hired Renault. 'Last night you drove too fast along such a narrow road, Portia. Perhaps,' he added, looking her in the eye, 'because you know it well?'

'Yes, I do,' she agreed, and got into the car.

When they reached Turret House Luc Brissac parked the car on the gravel terrace, reached into the back for a suede jacket and came round to let Portia out.

'It looks more welcoming today than last night,' he commented, eyeing the brick façade. 'Sunlight is kinder to it than—what is *crépuscule*?'

'Twilight,' said Portia, and unlocked the front door, ushering him ahead of her into the hall, where the sunlight cast coloured lozenges of light on the tiled floor, an effect which found favour with her client.

'Most picturesque,' he said, then smiled wryly. 'But I should not make favourable comments. I must frown and look disapproving so that you will drop the price.'

Portia smiled neutrally, and accompanied him through the ground-floor rooms again, glad to see that daylight failed to show up any flaws her tension might have blinded her to the previous evening. Luc paused in each room to make notes, keeping Portia on her toes with pertinent, informed questions right up to the moment they reached the tower and she could no longer ignore the faint, familiar dread as he opened the door to the ground-floor sitting room.

'If you do not wish to go as far as the top floor again you need not, Portia,' he said quickly. His eyes, a very definite green this morning in the light streaming through three sets of windows, held hers questioningly.

She shook her head, exerting iron control on her reactions. 'I'm fine. Really.' She ran swiftly up the spiral stairs to prove it, and went straight across the top room to the windows. 'As I told you, the view from up here is breathtaking.'

Luc Brissac studied her profile for a moment, then looked down at the tiered lawns and shrubberies of the garden, with its belt of woodland, and beyond that the cliff-edge and a glimpse of sandy cove below, and the sea glittering under the blue winter sky. He nodded slowly. 'You were right, Portia. For this, on such a day, one can almost forgive the excesses of the Turret House architect.'

Almost, noted Portia. 'You mentioned going down to the cove,' she reminded him. 'Do you have time for that?'

He nodded. 'Yes. Did I not say? I was able to postpone my departure until tomorrow. We can explore this cove at our leisure, then later we shall lunch together to discuss the transaction.'

Portia, not altogether pleased by his high-handed rearrangement of her day, opened the door into the lift and went in. Luc followed her, frowning as he pressed the button to go down.

'You feel I am monopolising too much of your time?' he asked.

'No.' He's the client, she reminded herself. 'If you want a discussion over lunch then of course I'll delay my return to London. But I shall pay for the meal.' She stepped out of the lift into the hall, and made for the door.

'Since lunch was my suggestion I shall pay,' he said loftily, following her.

She shook her head. 'I'll charge it to my expense account. And,' she added with emphasis, 'I suggest we lunch in a pub somewhere, not at the hotel.'

He stood outside on the terrace, arms folded, watching as she locked the door. 'You do not like the food at the hotel?'

'Of course. It's superb.' She led the way down a series of stone steps towards the bottom of the garden. 'But Ben Parrish says the meals are good at the Wheatsheaf, a couple of miles away, so I thought you might like some plain British fare for a change.'

Portia laughed at his undisguised look of dismay, and Luc smiled in swift response as they reached the path that led through the copse of trees to the cliff-edge. 'You should laugh more often, Portia.'

'Take care down here,' she said, turning away. 'It's pretty steep.' She went ahead of him down the overgrown path which cut down the cliffside in sharp bends to the cove below, with loose shale adding to the hazards in places.

Portia made the descent with the sure-footed speed of long practice. When Luc Brissac joined her a few minutes later he was breathing heavily, a look of accusation on his face.

'Such a pace was madness, Portia!'

She shook her head, and turned to look out to sea, shivering a little as she hugged her jacket closer. 'The path was quite safe.'

'For mountain goats at such speed, possibly. Or,' he added deliberately, 'for someone very familiar with it.' He waited a little, but when she said nothing he looked away, gazing about him in approval at the rocks edging the sand in the secluded, V-shaped inlet. 'But this is charming. Is there any other access?'

'No. The path is Turret House property.'

Luc turned up the collar of his suede jacket. 'In summer this must be delightful. A great asset to the house.'

'The path could do with some work,' admitted Portia. 'But if it's reinforced in places, with a few steps cut in the cliff here and there, and maybe a handrail on the steepest bit, it could be a very attractive feature. Not many houses boast a private cove.'

'True.' Luc cast an eye at clouds gathering on the horizon. 'Come, Portia, we must go back before it rains.'

Portia found the climb up the cliff far harder going than her reckless, headlong descent. By the time she reached the top she was out of breath. 'As I said yesterday,' she panted, as Luc joined her, 'I'm out of condition.'

His all-encompassing look rendered her even more breathless. 'Your condition looks flawless to me. Come. It is early yet for lunch, but perhaps your English pub will give us coffee.'

'If I'd known you weren't going back today I would have asked for a later start this morning,' said Portia as they went back up through the garden.

He shrugged. 'My change of plan took much effort to rearrange. I was not sure until this morning that it could be done.'

'Why did you change your mind?' she asked curiously, as they got in the car.

'There would not have been time before my flight to go down to the cove after inspecting the house again. And this was necessary before I made a decision.' He concentrated on the steep bends of the drive. 'Also,' he added casually, 'I desired to spend more time with you. Now, give me directions, please. Where is this inn of yours?'

The Wheatsheaf served excellent coffee, and later provided them with a simple, but well-cooked lunch very different from the cuisine at the Ravenswood, but in its own way of a very high standard.

'But this is very good!' pronounced Luc, as he ate roast lamb cooked with anchovies and garlic.

Portia laughed. 'The compliment would sound better without the astonishment.'

Luc grinned. 'We take our food more seriously than you British.'

'And suffer far less from heart problems, I read somewhere. Though you drink a bit more than we do,' she added, then regretted it at the look on Luc's face.

'True,' he said quietly.

'I didn't mean you personally, of course,' said Portia hurriedly.

'I know.' His smile stopped short of his eyes. 'You would like dessert?'

She shook her head.

'Then perhaps we can return to the bar to talk business. Please excuse me for a moment. I shall order coffee.' Luc seated her at a small table, then went off for a word with the barman.

Conscious of unintended transgression of some kind, Portia resolved to put a guard on her tongue for the rest of their time together. Luc had flatly refused to discuss Turret House before lunch, so her only opportunity for clinching a sale was during the short time left before her drive back to London. And outside, she noted glumly, the rain was coming down in torrents.

'You look pensive,' said Luc, as he rejoined her.

'I was eyeing the weather. I'm afraid I'll have to cut things short. It's a fair drive back to London.'

'I know.' He put a hand on hers. 'Stay the night at the Ravenswood again, Portia, and drive back in the morning.'

So, Jean-Christophe Lucien Brissac was no different from the rest after all. Portia removed her hand abruptly, utterly astounded by the discovery that she was deeply tempted to say yes.

'No, I can't do that,' she said quietly. 'I'm quite accustomed to long journeys in any weather. So, shall we discuss Turret House, or have you made your decision already?'

'I was not asking to share your room, Miss Grant,' he said icily. 'My concern was for your safety, only.'

'Of course.' Utterly mortified, Portia began packing her briefcase. 'I shan't rush you. I didn't expect a firm answer today, anyway. Perhaps you'll get in touch as soon as possible and let me know what you decide. In the meantime—'

'In the meantime, sit down and drink your coffee,' said Luc, with a note of command. 'You mistake me,' he added as she resumed her seat. 'Also you insult me.'

She frowned. 'Insult you?'

'Yes. It is not my habit to force my way into a woman's bed. Even a woman as alluring and challenging as you,' he informed her.

Portia calmed down a little. 'My apologies,' she said stiffly.

There was silence between them for a moment.

'You have been troubled by clients before?' Luc asked.

'No. My clients usually come in pairs.'

'By men in general, then?'

'One or two,' she said without inflection.

His eyes lit with wry sympathy. 'A woman with looks like yours—' He shrugged. 'It is easy to understand why.'

'If that's a compliment, thank you.'

He gave her a sidelong, considering look. 'It was meant to be. Though now, knowing that you suspect me of dark and devious motives, I shall strive to be careful.'

'Careful?' she said, frowning.

'That I do not offend.'

'I can't afford to be offended,' she said matter-of-factly. 'You're the client.'

His smile was tigerish. 'And you want me to buy a property that remains on your books rather a long time.'

So much for hoping to sell Turret House without a reduction. If she sold it at all. 'Of course I do,' she said, resigned.

Luc spent some time looking through the details of the house again, checking off various points against the notes he'd made. At last he turned to her with a businesslike air, raising his voice slightly above the crowded, post-prandial noise of the Wheatsheaf bar.

'I will consider my options most carefully, Portia, and then this evening, after your return to London, I shall ring you and let you know my decision,' he said with finality.

'If you're staying over tonight you can have longer

than that,' she said quickly, suppressing a leap of excitement. He was going to buy; she was sure of it. 'You can ring me at the office in the morning.'

He shook his head. 'Give me your phone number. I shall ring you tonight.'

Portia hesitated for a moment, then scribbled a number on a sheet from her diary and handed it to him.

'Thank you,' he said, and tucked it in his wallet. 'And now I will drive you back to Ravenswood.'

Outside, they raced through the rain to Luc's car. '*Mon Dieu*, what weather!' he gasped, as they fastened their seatbelts.

'It's not always like this,' she assured him breathlessly. 'The climate here is the best in the UK.'

'Not so *very* good a recommendation!'

Portia smiled, badly wanting a hint from him as to his decision about Turret House. But prudence curbed her tongue. If he sensed she was desperate to sell he would expect a substantial drop in the price. Assuming he did want the house. She eyed his profile searchingly, but it gave her no clue to his intentions.

When they reached the car park of the Ravenswood, Portia refused his invitation to go inside for a while before she started back to London.

'I'd rather go now and get it over with.'

'How long will the journey take?' he asked, frowning at the rain.

'I don't know. In this weather longer than usual, I'm afraid.'

'I shall ring you at ten. This will give you time?'

'I hope so.' Portia held out her hand. 'Thank you for the room, and my dinner—and for the lunch. When I tried to settle up just now they told me you'd already paid.'

He took the hand in his, shrugging. 'I never allow a woman to pay.'

'An attitude that gets you in trouble sometimes these days, I imagine?'

He looked surprised. 'Never—until now.' He raised her hand to his lips. '*Au 'voir*, Portia Grant. I shall talk to you later. Drive very carefully.'

'I always do. Goodbye.' She got in the car, fastened her seatbelt and drove off quickly, dismayed to find she already needed her headlights in the streaming February dusk. As she turned out into the road she looked in her mirror, rather disappointed that Luc Brissac hadn't waited to watch her out of sight. Not, she told herself severely, that there was any reason why he should. Only an impractical fool would have hung about in the drenching rain. And her acquaintance with Jean-Christophe Lucien Brissac might be slight, but one thing was very clear. He was no fool.

CHAPTER THREE

PORTIA'S return journey to London was nerve-racking. After a slow journey to the motorway, the rest of it was a nightmare of pouring rain and heavy spray from other vehicles, all three lanes clogged by traffic, all the way to London. When she reached Chiswick at last Portia felt exhausted. She parked her car in the basement garage, went up in the lift to her flat, locked her door behind her, then took her cellphone from her bag and blew out her cheeks in relief.

Now she was home and dry, she had an hour to spare before the call from the charming, disturbing Monsieur Brissac. If he confirmed he was going to buy Turret House it might be best to ask Ben Parrish to deal with him from now on.

A minute or so before ten the cellphone rang, right on cue, and she hit the button in sudden excitement.

'Portia Grant,' she said crisply.

'Ah, *bon*, you are returned safely,' said Luc Brissac with gratifying relief. 'I was worried, Portia.'

'How nice of you. But quite unnecessary. I've been home some time.'

'Then you did drive too fast!'

'I couldn't. Once I joined the motorway I was stuck in the middle lane all the way to London.'

'*Bien*, it is established that you arrived safely. So now, Portia, we get to business.'

'You've made a decision?' she asked, trying not to sound too eager.

36

'Yes. I confirm that I will buy Turret House. But,' he added emphatically, 'only on certain conditions.'

Portia's flare of triumph dimmed a little. 'What conditions do you have in mind?'

'First the price.' He named a figure lower than she'd hoped, but higher than the reduction Whitefriars had been about to recommend to the vendors.

'I must consult my partners, of course, but I'm sure we can come to an agreement on that,' said Portia, secretly elated.

'Also,' he went on, 'I wish you, personally, to conduct the entire transaction.'

She frowned. 'But it's actually Mr Parrish's—'

'I want you, Portia,' he said with emphasis.

Or he wouldn't buy it. The words remained unspoken, but Portia, visualising his usual shrug, was left in no doubt.

'As you wish.'

'Next weekend I fly back to London. In the meantime I shall arrange for information about my lawyers to be faxed to you, also contact numbers where I can be reached until we meet again.'

'Thank you,' she said briskly, secretly thrilled at her success in getting rid of the property Ben Parrish had failed to move.

'Please arrange to leave next weekend free,' went on Luc Brissac.

She stiffened. 'Oh, but—'

'I wish to inspect the property again. I cannot take possession of the keys until the house is legally mine, Portia. You must come with me. I shall drive you down to Turret House early on Saturday morning.'

For a split-second Portia was tempted to tell him exactly what he could do with his conditions, *and* his pur-

chase of Turret House. But common sense prevailed.
'Monsieur Brissac, I shall do as you ask, but with a
condition of my own. I'll drive down to the house sep-
arately and meet you there.'

There was silence for a moment, then he sighed impatiently. 'Very well, if you insist. But please be there
by mid-morning.'

'Of course.'

'Until Saturday, then, Portia.'

The following morning her news of the sale of Turret
House was greeted with teasing surprise by her partners
at Whitefriars, and deep respect by Biddy, who was still
heavy-eyed and red-nosed, but slowly recovering from
her cold.

'I thought we'd never get rid of the place!' Biddy had
been with the firm for years and looked on every property sale as a personal triumph. She handed Portia a cup
of coffee and lingered expectantly, obviously wanting
details before she went off to start on the letters and
valuations Portia had gone through with her on the
Friday afternoon before sending her home to bed.

Before she'd ever heard of Luc Brissac, thought
Portia. 'The client wants me to go down to Turret House
again this weekend.'

'Was his wife with him?' asked Biddy.

'No, he's not married.'

'Then I'd better come with you.'

'No need,' said Portia quickly. 'But thanks for the
offer.'

'I thought Mr Parrish always took people round it anyway.'

'Monsieur Brissac insists on my personal attention for
the transaction,' said Portia. And, for reasons she pre-

ferred to keep to herself, she wanted to deal with this particular client on her own. She shot to her feet. 'Heavens, is that the time? I'm due in Belgravia in ten minutes to sell a pricey mews cottage to your favourite soap queen.'

When Ben Parrish got back from his skiing trip next day he was amazed to find Portia had managed to sell Turret House while he was away.

'Though I suppose I shouldn't be surprised. Luc Brissac probably took one look at you and said yes to anything you wanted.'

Ben Parrish was only a few years older than Portia, stocky, sandy-haired, and possessed of a solid brand of charm that stood him in good stead in the property business. Without ever resorting to the hard sell, he nevertheless managed to move properties at a rate envied by his colleagues at Whitefriars. But success with Turret House had eluded him.

'You know him, then?' asked Portia.

He nodded. 'I sold a place in Hampstead to him quite recently. He knows one of the partners is always on call on winter weekends.'

'So why didn't you tell me he was coming?'

'I thought he was due next weekend.' He consulted his diary. 'I'm right. He was supposed to come next Saturday, in which case I'd have taken him round the place. As I always do,' he added significantly.

'Yes, I know,' said Portia, softening. 'Anyway, he turned up last weekend, and also commands my presence down there next weekend as well. You owe me, Mr Parrish.''

Whitefriars Estates was a thriving business, which dealt with desirable properties at the top end of the market, all of them in fashionable, expensive locations. The

clients were often celebrities of one kind or another, and
Portia's day was rarely boring. The week progressed in
its usual way, other than a hiccup with her car. When
she took it in for a service she was told it needed parts
which wouldn't be available for a day or two, which
meant the car wouldn't be ready until late on Monday.

Portia travelled by Underground the rest of the week,
except for the evening she went straight from the office
to dine with Joe Marcus. Joe was a property developer
she'd met on her MBA course, a high-flyer, clever, with
a wicked sense of humour, and determined to avoid marriage until he was at least forty. He took Portia out regularly, secure in the fact that she shared his point of
view. And with Marianne in the throes of a new love
affair, Portia kept the other evenings free, to get as much
sleep as possible to prepare for another visit to Turret
House. And a meeting with Luc Brissac again. A prospect she found herself looking forward to more than she
wanted to admit.

On the Friday Portia snatched a half-hour at lunchtime
for a sandwich in her office. She was immersed in the
designs Biddy had prepared for a brochure, when her
cellphone rang. She eyed it for a moment. Marianne's
new idol probably had clay feet. Again. With a sigh, she
pressed the button.

'Portia?' said a voice with an unmistakable French
cadence. 'Luc Brissac.'

To her annoyance her heart missed a beat, then she
tensed, suddenly afraid he was going to pull out of the
deal. 'Hello. How are you?'

'Very well. I wish to confirm our appointment tomorrow.'

Portia let out a silent breath of relief. 'Good. Actually,

I'm glad you rang. I can't make it to the house until noon. Does that suit you?'

'It would suit me better to drive you there myself, Mademoiselle Portia.'

A little thrill of excitement ran through Portia. It was only practical to accept, she told herself firmly, now her car was out of action. The alternative was a train at the crack of dawn, and a taxi to take her to Turret House. Which would be sheer stupidity when she could enjoy the journey in the company of Luc Brissac.

'You are still there?' he asked. 'If you have an appointment tomorrow night do not worry. I will drive you back in time. Or are you only content when driving yourself, Portia?'

'No, of course not. Thank you. What time do you want to leave?'

'I shall pick you up at nine. Where do you live?'

'No need for that. I'll meet you somewhere.'

'I insist on coming to *you*, Portia. Your address, please.'

She hesitated, then told him where to collect her. 'I'll be ready at nine, then.'

'I look forward to seeing you again. *A demain*, Portia.'

Assuming Luc Brissac would want another climb down to the cove, Portia was ready well before nine next morning in sensible shoes, black sweater, black needle-cord trousers and her amber fleece jacket, shivering a little with combined cold and anticipation as she waited on the pavement.

When a Renault came to a halt at the kerb Luc Brissac jumped out, smiling. 'Portia—you should not be standing outside in such weather.'

'Good morning.' She smiled. 'I thought I'd save some time.'

Luc was dressed casually again, in suede windbreaker, cashmere sweater and elegantly battered cords, none of it any different from some of the men she knew. The difference, she decided, lay in nationality, and his air of supreme self-confidence.

'You look delightful this morning, Portia,' he remarked as he drove off. 'Did your week go well?'

'Socially and professionally very well indeed.' Portia smiled wryly. 'The only blot on my week was my car. It needed a bigger repair than expected.'

'Ah.' Luc sent a gleaming look in her direction before negotiating a busy roundabout. 'So this is why you so meekly allow me to drive you to Turret House?'

'Yes,' she said demurely, and he laughed.

'You are so bad for my self-esteem, Portia Grant. Could you not pretend you joined me for the sake of my company on the journey?'

'I don't do pretence,' she informed him. 'But I'll admit I'm very grateful for a lift. I didn't enjoy the drive home last Sunday.'

'I was most concerned. It was a long evening before I could ring to assure myself that you were safe,' he informed her.

Portia gave him a surprised look. 'How very nice of you.'

'Nice? Such British understatement!' He shook his head in amusement. 'Now. Tell me. What expensive properties did you sell this week, Portia? Is business good?'

Portia told him business was surprisingly good for the time of year. The rest of the journey was spent in easy conversation more concerned with the property market and current affairs than any personal details on either side, which Portia found rather intriguing. Usually her male companions were only too ready to talk about themselves. The journey seemed much shorter than usual, and all too soon, it seemed to Portia, they came to the familiar crossroads and took the fork to Turret House.

The day was grey and cold, and without the sunshine of the week before the house looked even less inviting as Luc parked the car outside the Gothic arch of the front door.

'It needs trees in pots and tubs filled with flowers to soften the effect of the brick,' said Portia, getting out.

This time, with Luc for company, it was easier to unlock the door and go inside. Portia snapped on the lights quickly, but before following her Luc turned back to the car and took two folded director's chairs from the boot, then reached in again for a picnic basket. 'This time we drink our coffee here,' he announced.

Portia eyed the basket in surprise. 'That's very big for just coffee.'

He smiled. 'There is also a picnic for later, should you disapprove of lunch at Ravenswood. Since the kitchen is the only complete room, let us establish ourselves there.' He paused, chairs in one hand, the basket in the other. 'Unless you cannot bear to remain that long?'

'But I thought the whole idea of getting me down here today was to give you access to the place,' she said, frowning.

The green eyes met hers very directly. 'Part of the idea only, Portia.'

Portia turned away, surprised to find she no longer felt in the least uneasy with Luc Brissac. And in his company she was not as opposed to time spent in Turret House as he obviously assumed. 'Let's have that coffee, then.'

Luc placed the chairs near the window looking out over the back garden, then opened one flap of the basket and filled china beakers with coffee from a vacuum flask. He added milk from another flask to Portia's, and handed it to her with a bow.

'*Voilà*. That is the way you like it?'

'Yes, it is,' she said impressed. 'Thank you.' She sat down in one of the chairs, looking at him questioningly. 'Do you need any help with measurements, or anything like that?'

Luc smiled at her indulgently and shook his head. 'No. But it is most kind of you to offer.'

'Then why, exactly, am I here?' she asked.

'If *you* were not with me, legally I could not enter Turret House.'

Portia drank some of her coffee. 'Monsieur Brissac—'

'Luc,' he contradicted.

'Luc, then,' she said impatiently. 'I've given up a Saturday to come down here, so surely I'm entitled to know what you want me to do.'

'But I told you that last time we met.'

She looked at him narrowly. 'You've brought me all this way just to find out why I dislike Turret House?'

He shrugged. 'Partly. But surely it is obvious to you by this time that I also desire your company?'

She stiffened. 'You could have had that in London.'

'Could I, Portia?' he said swiftly. 'If I asked you out to a purely social dinner would you accept? *Non*, I think not. So this way you are obliged to suffer my company, also to keep your promise.'

Portia stared down into her coffee for a moment, then

looked up to meet the intent green eyes. 'As I said, I don't do pretence, so it's not a case of *suffering* your company.'

His eyes gleamed with open triumph. 'I am honoured, Portia. That was not easy for you to say, I think.'

'No,' she agreed, and smiled a little. 'It won't be easy to tell you what you want to know either, so I require something in return.'

'Anything you desire,' he said swiftly.

'I'm curious to know why you're buying Turret House.'

'*D'accord,*' he said promptly, then grinned. 'Better still, you can make guesses.'

'Right,' she said, feeling suddenly light-hearted. 'Let's see, you're getting married and intend to have a large family?'

He shook his head. 'Wrong, *mademoiselle*. Try again.'

Startled by how much his answer pleased her, Portia thought for a moment, then said, 'I've got it. You were interested in the elevator. You want the house for a retirement home!'

Luc chuckled. 'Wrong again.'

Portia threw up a hand. 'I give in.'

'The house is needed as an annexe for Ravenswood. Business there is brisk, and often the hotel is obliged to turn customers away. Turret House is only a mile or two away, and there could be transport from one place to the other. Also,' he added, 'the private cove is a great advantage for families with children.'

Portia smiled at him in delight. 'But that's a wonderful idea, Luc. It's exactly what the place needs, lots of life, with people coming and going.'

'I'm glad you agree.' He stood up. 'Come, let us make another inspection. You shall look at everything with the eye of a guest, and tell me if you approve my ideas. But afterwards,' he added with emphasis, 'I shall keep you to your promise.'

As though bent on banishing any lingering ghosts for Portia, the sun broke through the clouds as she went through the house with Luc again. This time, looking at it with an eye to its possibilities as a hotel annexe, the house took on a new personality to Portia as they discussed possible use for each of the rooms, and which alterations would be necessary before it could function as a hotel. She grew enthusiastic and animated, stray curls escaping round her face, but tailed into silence at last as she realised Luc was looking at her without listening to a word she was saying.

'What is it?' she asked suspiciously. 'Am I talking nonsense?'

'Some of your suggestions are very practical. They will be of much use.' He hesitated, then gave his familiar shrug. 'It is just that you are so beautiful like this, Portia—like a statue come to life. I am dazzled.' He grimaced as the animation faded from her face. 'I am also a fool. Now I have spoiled it all. You will demand to be returned to London at once.'

'No, I won't do that,' said Portia, secretly disarmed by the compliment. 'In any case you haven't seen everything yet. There's something I forgot to show you last week.'

'There is?' He looked at her warily. 'So. After you show me this you will share the picnic with me?'

'Yes, I will. I'm hungry.' She smiled at him mischievously, her eyes dancing, and Luc made an involuntary move towards her, then halted.

'Maybe,' he said with constraint, 'we should eat at Ravenswood—'

'No,' she said firmly.

'Or at the inn we went to last week.' His eyes met hers. 'But it was very noisy there, not a place easy for conversation.'

'True. So we'll picnic here—pity to waste the contents of that smart basket.'

He smiled. 'I am not sure what they are. I did not pack it.'

Portia felt a definite pang at the thought of some woman making up a picnic lunch for Luc Brissac. Hey, she told herself. He's just a client.

Portia led Luc back to the kitchen and out into a room used by the precious owners as a laundry. A door from it led out into a large porch, with an outer door into the garden, and another which Portia opened on a flight of steps leading downward. As she turned on the light Luc caught her by the arm.

'Is that a cellar? You need not go down there, Portia. I can explore alone.'

'I don't mind in the slightest,' she assured him, and led the way down to a large basement room which housed the oil-fired central heating boiler and rows of empty wine racks.

Luc looked at her searchingly as he joined her. 'The cellar holds no terror for you, then?'

'No,' she said cheerfully. 'There's not much to see down here, other than the boiler.'

He inspected it, frowning. 'This must be replaced. It cannot have served the entire house.'

'I suppose the vendors rarely needed heat in every room at the same time.'

Luc nodded, then waved her ahead of him. 'Let us go back to the kitchen and eat this lunch. I asked for something nourishing to suit the weather, so let us investigate.'

The picnic basket yielded more insulated flasks, containers filled with bread rolls and several types of cheese, plates, and silverware wrapped in starched white napkins.

'Because you might be cold I asked for lobster bisque,' said Luc, opening one of the flasks. 'It smells good. And I know you like lobster, Portia, because you ordered it for your dinner the other night. There is no wine, alas. So we must content ourselves with mineral water and coffee.'

'What exactly do you do, Luc?' she asked curiously as he filled fresh beakers with the soup. 'Are you a representative for a hotel chain?'

He nodded absently, intent on his task.

'That explains why you're so well known at the Ravenswood.'

He handed her a mug of soup. 'Try that, Portia.'

She sipped, and smiled at him. 'Delicious.'

Luc put the basket down between them on the kitchen floor. 'The easiest way, I think, without a table.'

They ate rolls and finished the flask of soup between them, talking over the improvements Luc felt were necessary for the success of Turret House.

'But I do not like the name,' he said, cutting a piece of Roquefort for her.

'Ravenswood Annexe? Or Cliff House?'

He shook his head. 'It does not ring the bell.'

'The house is near the edge of the cliff—Edgecliff?' She wrinkled her nose. 'Sounds like a Victorian novel. You need something romantic, inviting. My schoolgirl French isn't very wonderful, I regret to say. How do you say cliff-edge, Luc?'

'*Au bord de la falaise,*' he said, and Portia smiled triumphantly.

'Perfect! Plant creeper to soften the brick walls, and fill some urns with flowers, call the annexe La Falaise and Turret House will be a thing of the past.'

'As it was once part of your past, I think?' he said, his eyes questioning.

Portia nodded, suddenly sober. 'Yes. At one time it was my home.'

CHAPTER FOUR

'TIME to keep my promise.' Portia was silent for a moment, then she got up to rinse out their beakers. 'Could I have some coffee first?'

Luc frowned. 'Portia, I have changed my mind. Do not disturb yourself by telling me more. If they are painful, leave your memories in the past.'

She hesitated, almost tempted to agree. But in some strange way she felt she owed Luc Brissac something for laying her ghosts—unknowingly, it was true. But if he hadn't demanded her presence at Turret House she would never have set foot in it again, and it would have continued to haunt her. Now the ghosts were exorcised. The proof of this was the very fact that she was picnicking here in the Turret House kitchen. A situation she would have laughed to scorn if anyone had predicted it.

'I've psyched myself up to it now,' she said, as Luc poured coffee from a fresh flask. 'And we made a deal. My past isn't something I discuss much, but if you'd like to hear about it I'm willing to tell you.' She smiled faintly. 'It's supposed to be easier to confide in strangers.'

Luc gave her an unexpectedly cold look. 'Is that how you think of me, Portia? As a stranger?'

Her eyes fell. 'If I'm honest, I've done my best to think of you solely as a client.'

'You have done your best, you say?' repeated Luc thoughtfully. 'Does that mean you did not find it easy? To think of me as just a client?'

Portia looked at him warily, not sure how to answer, and he smiled.

'*Alors*, Portia. Begin at the beginning. Were you born here?'

She shook her head. 'I come from a small village about twenty miles away. I lived in a house attached to my father's garage—a small place that did car repairs.'

'Of course! Your father named you for the Porsche.'

She smiled ruefully. 'Not that he ever owned one.'

'And your mother?'

'She was a born home-maker, a fabulous cook and very pretty. My father adored her—wouldn't hear of her getting a job, even though money was always tight. Dad was brilliant at his craft, but hopeless about getting people to settle their bills. When I won a scholarship to the local girls' school they were so delighted and proud.' Portia paused to clear her throat, and Luc put out a hand to touch hers.

'Do you want to go on?'

'Yes. You may as well know the rest.' She took in a deep breath. 'When I was fourteen my father was out test-driving a car he'd repaired. A drunken idiot in a pick-up jumped a red light and rammed into him. Dad died later in hospital.'

'*Mon Dieu!*' Luc moved his chair closer and took her hand firmly in his.

Comforted by his touch, Portia did her best to keep to the unvarnished facts as she told him that the garage had been losing money, there'd been a second mortgage on the house, and Christine Grant had been left virtually penniless.

'It was so terrible for her.' Portia swallowed hard. 'She was in despair, until Mr Radford came up with a solution.'

Lewis Radford had been the solicitor in charge of Paul Grant's affairs. He'd lived alone at Turret House, his housekeeper had wanted to retire, and in the circumstances he'd suggested Christine Grant might care to take her place.

'So we came here to live,' said Portia colourlessly.

'This man was unkind to you?' demanded Luc.

'No. I hardly ever saw him. I was told to keep out of sight and never disturb him.' Portia shivered. 'So Mother and I had security, but we both missed Dad so horribly and the first year was grim. I was so miserable I put on weight and came out in spots.'

'This is hard to believe!'

'I turned to junk food for comfort.' Portia smiled wryly. 'Then a new girl arrived at the school. Marianne was blonde, pretty, and great fun. We were opposites in every way, but we hit it off right from the first. My life—and my appearance—improved enormously. Then at eighteen I went off to Reading to study Land Management. Mr Radford, much to our surprise, offered financial help.'

'And your friend?'

'Marianne went to Oxford to read English. We kept in touch, always, but after her family moved to Kent there was no one here for me in the vacations. So in warm weather I spent most of my free time down in the cove.'

Luc released her hand abruptly and stood up to pour more coffee. 'I assume,' he said after a while, 'that you slept in the room at the top of the tower.'

'Heavens, no. Mother and I had tiny adjoining rooms upstairs at the back, bathrooms now. The tower was Mr Radford's private property. He used the first two floors as a sitting room and a study, but the top floor was kept locked. Not even my mother was allowed up there. When I first came here I had nightmares about it, imagined all sorts of horrors.'

'Did you eventually discover the secret of the locked room?' asked Luc.

Portia managed a smile. 'That sounds like the title of a Sherlock Holmes mystery.'

'I confess I am intrigued.'

'My mother said Mr Radford kept confidential files for special clients there.' She was silent for a while, her eyes heavy with memories.

'So, Portia,' Luc prompted eventually, 'you achieved your degree?'

'Yes. But soon afterwards my mother died...' She trailed into silence, fighting a losing battle with tears. She took a tissue from her bag and scrubbed at her eyes. 'Shortly afterwards,' she continued hoarsely, getting up, 'Mr Radford died too. He'd left my mother some money, and it came to me. End of story.'

Luc took her hands in his. 'Ah, *chérie*, do not cry. Was this money enough to make life bearable for you?'

The endearment seemed so natural Portia hardly noticed it. 'It meant that with a lot of economising I could wait for a while before the right job came along and when I'd gained enough experience I still had just enough money left to take time off to study for my MBA—my Masters in Business Administration,' she added.

He nodded. 'I studied for this also. It is a demanding course.'

'Without it I wouldn't be a partner—though a very junior one—at Whitefriars.' She turned away. 'There. The story of my life.'

'Not all of it, Portia.'

'No, not quite. The rest is pretty ordinary. Boring, even.' She began repacking the picnic basket.

'You could never bore me, Portia,' Luc assured her.

'You haven't spent enough time with me to be sure of that,' she said, and turned to smile at him.

'A situation I intend to remedy.' He touched a fingertip to the tearstains under her eyes. 'Ah, *mignonne*,' he whispered, and took her into his arms. For a long, timeless interval he held her lightly, and Portia leaned against him pliantly, liking the comfort of the embrace as his hand stroked her hair. But at last, with supreme confidence of his welcome, Luc bent to kiss her, his lips meeting hers with tenderness which quickly transformed to heat as his arms tightened, and she responded instinctively for a moment or two before summoning the strength to free herself.

'Is this why you insisted I came here today?' she asked unevenly, backing away.

Luc stared at her in disbelief, then his face hardened. 'No, it is not! If you are implying that a sexual encounter was my aim, *mademoiselle*, I could have achieved that without leaving Paris. My sole intention,' he added caustically, 'was to make certain that this property would be suitable for the purpose I described to you.' He shrugged. 'But your story was touching. My urge was to comfort you. An impulse I now regret.'

After that there seemed little more to say. By the time Portia had visited a bathroom and tidied herself up Luc was waiting in the car with such hostile impatience she cursed herself for confiding in him.

For the first few miles of the journey the silence in the car was so impenetrable there was no possibility of breaking it even if Portia had wished to. The brief sunlight of noon had given way to a cold, grey afternoon, with the threat of fog. It matched her mood. Luc's too, she thought, depressed, wishing now she'd made less of the incident and passed off the kiss with more finesse.

They reached the motorway before Luc spoke.

'You need not worry,' he said brusquely, his accent more pronounced than usual. 'I shall keep my word.'

Portia glanced at his taut, imperious profile in surprise, then turned her gaze back on the myriad of red tail-lights stretching ahead of them. 'Good. Though I don't imagine my story would interest anyone else.'

'I meant my purchase of Turret House. But, since you mention it,' he added curtly, 'your confidences are also safe with me.'

'Oh.' Her cheeks burned. The possibility of losing the sale had never occurred to her. 'Thank you, Monsieur Brissac,' she said formally. 'On both counts.'

'You told me less about yourself than I wanted,' he said, sounding less hostile.

'My mission was to help with the house, not bore you to death.'

'You could never do that,' he assured her. 'Yours is a sad story, Portia.'

'Not any more,' she assured him.

He gave her a swift, sidelong glance. 'There is some man who makes you happy?'

'Yes,' she said with truth. Her weekly outings with Joe were great fun. He made her laugh, so it followed that he made her happy.

'Is it because of this man you were so reluctant to give up your weekend?' asked Luc, then broke off to curse volubly as a car cut in front of him without warning. 'Well?' he persisted later. 'Was your man angry that you spent the time with me?'

'Clients often take up my time at weekends,' Portia assured him. 'Joe understands perfectly.'

'So admirable,' said Luc Brissac with sarcasm. 'In his position I would not be so understanding.'

'Business is business,' said Portia, and slid further down in her seat and closed her eyes.

As a hint it was effective. Luc Brissac made no more attempt at conversation. Instead he switched on the radio and found a Vivaldi recital.

'I apologise for disturbing you,' he said later, long after Vivaldi had given way to Ravel. 'We are nearing London. I shall need directions to your apartment when we leave the *autoroute*.'

She sat up, yawning, doing her best to behave like someone waking from a deep sleep. 'Sorry. I was a bit tired.'

'You were out late last night?'

'No. I just didn't get to sleep very early.'

'This man lives with you?' he demanded.

Portia glared at him. 'No. He doesn't.' Then her eyes widened as she saw the familiar green sign looming up. 'Watch out—we get off at this exit.'

Cursing under his breath, Luc slammed a hand on the horn, and with negligent panache shot across the lanes of traffic down the slipway, braking so suddenly at the stop sign that the car behind shunted into them and Portia let out a screech as her temple hit the side window.

Luc killed the engine and pounced to release her seatbelt, blood trickling down his chin, his English deserting him as he bent over her in a frenzy of anxiety.

'Speak English, please,' she muttered.

'Are you much injured, Portia?' he demanded. '*Mon Dieu*, you are so pale.'

'I feel pale,' she said bitterly, and sat up, putting a hand to her throbbing head. 'Who's that outside, talking to the police?'

'It must be the driver who crashed into me,' said Luc with indifference. He dabbed at his mouth with a handkerchief, and, once Portia had managed to convince him she was relatively unhurt, got out of the car.

By the time names and addresses had been exchanged, and Luc, to his outrage, had been breathalysed by the police for his alcohol level, Portia had the worst headache of her entire life. She assured the police that she was in no need of an ambulance, and promised to see a doctor if she felt worse when she got home.

Luc assured them with arrogance that his companion would receive every care, and only Portia's hasty intervention averted an international incident when the policeman suggested that better care of the lady should have been taken in the first place.

When both cars were pronounced fit to drive, and they were finally allowed on their way, Luc put out a hand to touch Portia's. 'I ask your forgiveness.'

'Put your hand back on the wheel,' she gasped.

He obeyed promptly, sending a smouldering look at her. 'You cannot endure my slightest touch?'

'It isn't that,' she snapped. 'I'd just rather we got home in one piece.'

'Normally I am a very safe driver,' he said furiously. 'If you had told me which exit we took I would have been prepared.'

'All right, all right, I'm to blame,' she said irritably. 'Turn right at the next junction, please.'

Luc drove with exaggerated care for the rest of the way, and when they arrived handed Portia out of the car as if she were made of glass. 'Are you feeling better?'

he demanded. 'You must see a doctor at once. You could
be suffering concussion—'

'I've got a headache, Luc, that's all,' she said flatly.
'I'll make myself some tea and go straight to bed, and
I'll be fine.'

'I shall ring you later—' he began.

'Please don't—there's no need,' she said swiftly.
'Goodnight.'

'I will see you safely to your apartment,' he insisted.

Desperate for privacy and bed, Portia reminded herself
that Luc Brissac was a valued client, and let him go up
with her in the lift. When it stopped she held out her
hand. 'There. Safe and sound.'

Luc lifted the hand to his lips. 'I am so desolated that
the day should end in such a way. *Au 'voir*, Portia.'

She frowned as she noticed he was still bleeding from
the corner of his mouth. 'Does it hurt?' she asked.

He shrugged, and gave her a sardonic smile. 'Less
than my pride.'

When it became obvious that Luc Brissac was determined to wait until she was safely through the door,
Portia unlocked it, gave him a weary little smile and
closed the door on him.

Then she turned to face two people who rose from the
sofa to eye her in blank astonishment.

'Darling, do knock next time,' said Marianne, laughing. 'We could have been doing all sorts of sinful things
instead of watching television. This is Hal Courtney, by
the way. Hal, meet Portia Grant.'

'How do you do?' said Portia, as a strong hand
clasped hers. She smiled up into a thin, interesting face,
then muttered an apology and made for the bathroom at
speed.

After she'd parted with her lunch, washed her face,
drunk some water, and explored the bump on her temple,

Portia examined her discolouring eye with resignation, then went back to the living room, where Marianne had a tea tray ready, and Hal was nowhere to be seen.

'He tactfully took himself to the off-licence to get some wine for our supper. Now then, Portia, what *have* you been up to? You look ghastly.' Marianne fixed her with a steely blue gaze. 'And, not that it isn't lovely to see you, but for a moment there Hal thought someone was breaking and entering. You could have rung first.'

'I didn't mean to get as far as actually coming in,' said Portia, accepting a cup of tea. 'Thanks. I need this.'

'You've hurt yourself!' exclaimed Marianne, and turned Portia's face to the light. 'I didn't notice when you made your dramatic entry. What on earth happened to you?'

Portia gave a brief account of the day, and the circumstances which had led up to the bump on the head and the ensuing encounter with the police.

'Good heavens, darling,' said Marianne, aghast, 'are you sure you're all right? Shouldn't you go to a hospital to get checked?'

'That's what Luc Brissac wanted, but I'm fine. I just wanted to get home.'

'Who's Luc Brissac?'

'The man who's buying Turret House.' Portia met her friend's astonished stare with a grimace. 'That's right. Turret House. We were driving back from it when it happened. I was showing him round. He's going to buy it.'

Marianne leaned forward urgently and took her hand. 'You've actually been back to Turret House? Why didn't you *tell* me?'

'I meant to, but I knew you were busy with the new man—who seems very nice, by the way, from my fleeting glimpse.' Portia grinned. 'Time enough for girl-talk when you're at a loose end again.'

'That may be longer this time,' muttered Marianne.

Portia watched in awe. 'You're blushing!'

'It's not against the law, Portia Grant.' Marianne released her hand and sat back. 'And you wouldn't have interrupted anything.'

'Why not?'

'Because he's not like the others. We talk all the time, and enjoy just being together, doing things other people do. Walking, watching television, going to the cinema. Ordinary things.' She smiled radiantly. 'It's lovely.'

Portia was impressed. Marianne's men were usually the kind who wined and dined her expensively and expected return for their outlay. 'I'm glad,' she said simply. 'Sorry I barged in like that.'

'Don't be silly. But before I expire with curiosity, *please* tell me why it was necessary!'

'I didn't want Luc Brissac to know where I lived.'

Marianne sighed impatiently. 'Why ever not? Honestly, Portia, that flat of yours might just as well be an anchorite's cell.'

'Don't exaggerate. I hand my address out sparingly, that's all.' Portia shrugged. 'Luc Brissac is just a business connection. If he wants to contact me he can ring the office.'

'Is he nice?'

Portia thought about it. 'I don't think "nice" fits him, somehow.'

'Loaded, then. If he's buying Turret House he must have the odd penny or two.'

'He represents a hotel chain. He wants the house for an annexe to Ravenswood.'

Marianne frowned. 'What's his full name?'

'Jean-Christophe Lucien Brissac—' Portia winced.

'Have you got any painkillers, Marianne? I've got a splitting headache.'

The doorbell rang and Marianne jumped up to let Hal Courtney in. 'Why didn't you use your key?' she asked him as he came in with a clinking package of bottles.

'I was trying to be tactful,' he said, chuckling. 'I wasn't sure you'd want your friend to know I had a key.'

Portia smiled. 'As you saw, I've got one myself. Marianne keeps one of mine, too. Sorry I came crashing in on you earlier.'

'Talking of crashing,' said Marianne, 'give her the once-over, would you, Hal?'

'What's the problem? Trust me, Portia,' he added, eyes twinkling. 'I'm a doctor.'

After Portia explained about the incident in the car, Hal produced a medical bag and gave her a thorough examination, feeling her pulse and holding up a finger as he shone a slim torch beam in her eyes and asked if she felt sick.

'I threw up when I arrived, and I still feel a bit queasy,' she admitted apologetically, 'but the headache's the major problem.'

He pushed back unruly fair hair, eyeing her thoughtfully. 'I'm not surprised, Portia. You've got mild concussion.' He looked up into Marianne's anxious face. 'Could you rustle up some plain biscuits, darling? Once Portia's got them down, with some weak tea, I'll give her a couple of mild painkillers.'

Despite Portia's protests about ruining their evening, Marianne made her stay until her headache eased and she felt up to walking back to her flat. When Portia's phone rang just as they were ready to leave Marianne snatched it from her.

'Yes, she's here. I'm a friend. She's feeling very unwell.' She pulled a face and handed over the phone. 'It's a Monsieur Brissac,' she said very clearly.

'Hello,' said Portia, resigned.

'Your friend says you are ill,' said Luc heatedly. 'I should have taken you to a doctor—'

'I've seen a doctor. Apparently I've got slight concussion.'

'*Mon Dieu!* I am so sorry, Portia—'

'I'll be fine,' she assured him. 'By the way, how's your mouth?'

'It is why I did not ring earlier. My teeth caused damage to my lip. I needed a stitch,' he said with deep disgust. 'It would not stop bleeding.'

'Bad luck. I hope it's better soon. Goodnight.' She switched off the phone and put it in her bag, swaying a little.

'Steady the buffs,' said Hal, taking her arm. 'Are you sure you can walk? I've got the car.'

'I live in the next road,' said Portia. 'A walk would do me good.'

'We'll come with you,' said Marianne firmly.

'Oh, please don't—I'll be fine!'' said Portia in dismay, but nothing could dissuade either Hal or Marianne until she was back in the sanctuary of her own flat.

'This Brissac man's got a very sexy voice; I love his accent,' said Marianne, as they kissed goodnight. 'Why won't you give him your address?'

'I told you. He's strictly business.'

'Pity.'

'Get to bed right away, Portia,' said Hal. 'And see your own doctor tomorrow.'

Marianne sighed ecstatically. 'He's so masterful—I just love it!'

Hal shook his head, chuckling, put his arm round her and pushed her into the waiting lift. As the doors closed on them Portia was left with an indelible picture of Marianne gazing blissfully into the eyes laughing down into hers.

Annoyed because she felt vaguely sorry for herself, Portia closed her door and ran herself a bath. When she got into bed at last, her aching head propped up on several pillows, she wondered how Luc Brissac was feeling at this moment. Feigning sleep in the car had been a bad move. If she'd pointed out the exit in good time Luc's death-defying dash through the traffic would have been unnecessary. Now the man was mortified, and his ego badly dented. Not that it mattered. She was home in one piece, and, even more important, Turret House was now out of her life for good. Probably Luc Brissac's minions would work on the rest of the transaction. She need never see him again.

Portia frowned, rather startled to find she regretted this. Luc was attractive, sophisticated, and his insistence on seeing her again had been flattering. Nevertheless, there was a faint, indefinable something about him that made her uneasy. Which was illogical. Far from threatening her in any way he'd set out to charm from their first encounter in the hall at Turret House. And, if she were totally honest with herself, for a moment his kiss had been as welcome as he'd expected it to be. She sighed irritably. One way and another life would be more peaceful if Luc Brissac played no part in hers in future.

CHAPTER FIVE

PORTIA stayed in bed until the telephone woke her next morning. She picked up the receiver and yawned a response, her voice foggy with sleep.

'Wake up!' said Marianne urgently.

'I am awake. More or less. What's wrong?'

'I've just received a visit from a very irate Frenchman armed with roses. He's on his way round to you as we speak.'

'Mari*anne*,' shrieked Portia. 'How could you?'

'Very easily. He's gorgeous. I'll have words with you later, Portia Grant. Bye.'

Head protesting, Portia leapt out of bed, splashed water on her face, pulled on jeans and a jersey, and tied her hair back with a scarf. When her buzzer rang she cast a despairing look in the bathroom mirror and hurried to pick up the receiver.

'Luc Brissac,' he snapped. 'I wish to see you.'

'Come up, then.'

When Portia opened the door her heart sank as Luc, eyes blazing, thrust a vast bunch of tawny roses in her arms and stalked after her into the room, very obviously in a towering rage.

He stopped dead as the winter sunlight fell on her face. '*Mon Dieu*, you have a black eye!'

'How observant of you,' she said militantly. 'What lovely flowers. Thank you. I'll just put them in water.'

She took her time in the kitchen, looking for something large enough to hold several dozen long-stemmed blooms. In the end she put them in the sink, ran water into it, and returned to find Luc pacing up and down the room.

'Why did you play such silly games with me?' he demanded. 'Did it amuse you to make me feel like an idiot at your friend's apartment? The apartment,' he added, eyes kindling, 'that I escorted you to last night in the belief that it was yours!'

Portia looked away. 'I prefer to keep my address private.'

'And not only your address,' he said furiously. 'I just checked the number on your telephone. It is not the number you gave me. Does that also belong to your friend?'

'I gave you my cellphone number.' Portia tried a conciliatory smile. 'Won't you sit down?'

'No, I will not.' Luc flung over to the window and glowered at the view. 'I arrived at your friend's place this morning as one of the other tenants was leaving, so I was not obliged to ring a bell to gain entry. Otherwise, of course, I would have found your name missing from the list outside. So I rang the bell of the apartment I so stupidly believed was yours, and a man opened the door to me.' He swung round to glare at her. 'Can you imagine my reaction?'

Since Portia could imagine the scene only too clearly, she had trouble in keeping a straight face as she thought of Hal Courtney confronted with a strange man bearing roses. After his first night actually spent with Marianne, by the sound of it, too, she realised guiltily.

'You think this is amusing?' He muttered something French and unintelligible under his breath. 'I do not. Nor did your friend's lover. Naturally I believed he was the man you talk about. Now, of course, I know that the flat

belongs to your friend Marianne, and it was a Dr
Courtney who mistook me for a rival.'

Portia bit her lip. 'I'm sorry you were embarrassed,
but I never dreamed you'd call round in person.'

'I was responsible for causing you injury,' he said
through his teeth. 'Did you really believe I would just
go back to Paris and never give you another thought?'

'If I'd thought of it at all I'd have expected you to
send flowers, not bring them yourself.'

He glared at her. 'So. Once you sent me away yesterday you dismissed me from your mind!'

'*No,*' she retorted, suddenly angry herself. 'I meant I
didn't expect anything at all. Other than a phone call,
perhaps, to ask how I was.'

'You credit me with that much courtesy, then? *Merci!*'
he said bitingly. 'But you do not allow me to know your
address. Why? Do you dislike me so much?'

'No, of course not. It was nothing personal. Oh, do
sit down,' she added impatiently.

When Luc, not without some reluctance, took the
other end of the sofa she noticed a bruise along his jaw,
near the neatly stitched cut at the corner of his mouth.
'Nothing personal,' he repeated, and shrugged. 'You are
so bad for me, Portia Grant.'

She looked away. 'I haven't lived here long. As you
can see by the lack of furniture. It costs a lot to live
alone in London in a place like this. And I tend to keep
it to myself. No—please don't take offence,' she added
as his eyes narrowed ominously. 'All my life I've lived
with other people in one way or another. It was uphill
work to save enough money for a place of my own when
I can be completely private.' Portia looked at him in
appeal. 'I never thought I'd see you again after yesterday, anyway.'

'So you pretended your friend's apartment was yours.' Luc frowned. 'But you had a key. I saw you unlock the door, and open it.'

'She keeps one of my keys, too. It's a habit of ours.'

Luc raised an eyebrow. 'Your friend must have been surprised when you arrived so unexpectedly yesterday?'

'Yes. Especially as I had to rush to the bathroom right away to throw up.' She flushed, wishing she'd kept that particular detail to herself.

He frowned. 'This was the result of the blow?'

'Either that or pure fright. Luckily Hal Courtney's a doctor, so he saved Marianne the trouble of hauling me off to hospital. Which she would have done, otherwise.'

'As I wished to do,' he reminded her, then looked her in the eye. 'Tell me, Portia. Is this man of yours allowed to know where you live?'

'Yes.'

Luc gave the elegant little snort she was getting to know. 'Then I suppose I am fortunate that he did not answer your door to me and take exception to the roses also.'

Portia let out an irrepressible giggle. 'Sorry,' she said unsteadily, 'but I would have loved to be there when Hal Courtney found you on Marianne's doorstep.'

'*I* was not pleased to be there,' he retorted, but after a moment he smiled unwillingly. 'You are right. It is amusing to look back on. It was not at the time.'

Portia's eyes danced. 'It was the first time Hal's ever stayed the night with Marianne, too.'

'*Mon Dieu*—no wonder he looked ready to kill me!'

'I'm sorry I caused you such embarrassment, Luc,' she said penitently.

'If it was the only means to learn your address I shall

survive, Portia.' His eyes met hers. 'Are you nervous now I know where you live?'

'Should I be?' she countered. 'You don't live in England, after all.'

'Not all the time,' he agreed, suddenly very much in command of himself again. 'But I own an apartment in London.'

'Do you come over often, then?'

'I do much business here, so I come often enough to need a base. Perhaps very often in future,' he added.

'I see.'

'No, you do not see,' he assured her. 'Tell me, would this man of yours object to this?'

Portia's eyes narrowed. 'Object to what, exactly?'

'To your friendship with me.' Luc's eyes held hers, like a cat about to pounce. He leaned forward and lifted her left hand. 'You wear no ring, so he is not your fiancé, Portia.'

'Maybe not. But I don't suppose he'd take kindly to the idea.' Which was an out and out lie. Joe Marcus took Portia's socialising with other men for granted. Which suited her perfectly. She had no desire for a close relationship with any man. Certainly not Luc Brissac. But an inner voice told her she wasn't being entirely honest with herself on that point. Luc was a type of man new in her experience. Which probably accounted for the odd feeling of unease he aroused in her. Not that the feeling was dislike. Or physical repulsion. His kiss, fleeting though it had been, had demonstrated that only too clearly.

'You are very quiet,' he remarked. 'Do you wish me to leave?'

'Don't you have a plane to catch?'

He shook his head. 'Not until tomorrow.'

She waved a hand at his formal suit. 'But you must have an appointment somewhere, dressed like that?'

'My other clothes were stained with blood.' He smiled smugly. 'And to be dressed formally was a great advantage at your friend's apartment. Dr Courtney was wearing only a bathtowel.'

Portia shook her head, laughing, then winced as her bruise protested. 'Oh dear, oh dear. How I *wish* I'd been there.' She pulled a face. 'But I'll have some explaining to do to Marianne.'

'Why?'

She gave him a wry little smile. 'I said I was with a client when I got the bump on my head, but I didn't give any details, so she wasn't curious about you personally, only the fact that you were buying Turret House. Now she's met you, of course, it's another story.'

He frowned. 'In what way? She did not seem to object to me.'

Portia grinned mischievously. 'I bet she didn't. She finds your accent irresistible, she tells me. You obviously bowled Marianne over.'

'If so I am flattered,' he said, frowning. 'But, although she is a beautiful lady, and no doubt very charming, I do not—'

'I meant she probably thinks of you in relation to me,' said Portia, looking away. 'She's not terribly keen on Joe.'

Luc chuckled. 'Ah! You mean she likes making matches for you.'

'Something like that.'

'So she, at least, would be pleased if I asked to see you when I come to London?'

'That's not the point. It's *my* feelings you should be worrying about.'

'And I am,' he said swiftly. 'Otherwise why should I take so much trouble to find you? I was most reluctant to leave you last night. But I could not force you to let me stay. Also I was beginning to feel a little strange myself by that time.'

'So where did you get treatment?'

'I met one of my neighbours in the lift at my building. He was much concerned at the sight of me, and insisted on driving me to a hospital,' Luc shrugged. 'It was unnecessary, but without the stitch there would have been a scar, the doctor informed me.'

'Would that have worried you?'

His eyes gleamed sardonically. 'From a cosmetic point of view, not at all. But it occurred to me that if the cut was slow to get better I would not be able to kiss anyone.' The black-lashed eyes narrowed with a look that quickened her pulse. 'And even as you look now, *chérie*, with that regrettable black eye, the urge to kiss you is so strong it is a miracle I am so tamely keeping my distance.'

Portia felt colour flood into her face, and she jumped to her feet, which was a mistake, since Luc rose swiftly to bar her way. He stared down into her eyes, then took her in his arms.

'Do not be afraid,' he muttered into her hair, and tightened his hold as though expecting her to pull away. 'Yesterday you pushed me away.'

'I know,' she said into his shirt-front.

'Today is different?'

'It appears to be.'

Luc put a finger under her chin and lifted her bruised face to his, a wry smile twisting his injured mouth. 'Next weekend,' he said huskily, 'my stitch will be gone. If I fly over on Saturday, will you dine with me, Portia? Or will this man of yours object?'

'I'm my own woman, Luc,' she said with emphasis. 'If I want to dine with you I shall.'

His eyes glittered. 'And do you?'

She thought about it for a moment. 'Ring me later in the week.'

He scowled blackly. 'Why can you not say yes right now?'

Portia gave him a crooked little smile. 'Because I'm not dining out anywhere with a black eye, Luc Brissac. I do have my pride. So if you ring me on Friday I'll let you know if I'm fit to be seen.'

'I care nothing for your black eye.'

'Possibly not. But I do,' she said firmly, and smiled up at him.

'Mon Dieu,' he breathed, closing his eyes. 'I want to kiss you so much, Portia.'

'I could kiss you,' she offered, surprising herself.

Luc's eyes flew open, staring down into hers in disbelief.

'I'll be very careful,' she promised, and reached up to place her mouth at the corner of his, where she couldn't hurt him.

Luc stood like a man undergoing torture, his eyes tightly shut as her mouth moved over his cheek, and touched the bruise on his jaw with exquisite gentleness. With a stifled groan he put her away from him, breathing unevenly as he looked down at her flushed face.

'I was angry when I arrived,' he muttered.

'I know.'

'I thought you disliked me so much you would not even tell me where you lived.' He let out a deep, unsteady breath. 'Whereas I—'

'Whereas you?' prompted Portia.

''I do not dislike you,' he said in a constricted voice. 'But if I say more—as you well know I wish to do—you will refuse to see me again.'

Portia was surprised to find how unlikely that was. Now. It must be the knock on the head, she decided. It was by no means a habit of hers to kiss any man of her own accord. But his protective embrace had been strangely seductive.

'No,' she said quietly. 'I don't think I'll do that.'

'*Bon*. I am pleased.' Luc's eyes locked with hers. 'I must warn you, Portia, that it is only our respective wounds that force me to such restraint.'

Portia looked at him in silence for a moment. 'Are you saying,' she said slowly, 'that you will expect to sleep with me afterwards if I accept your invitation to dinner?'

He stood very still, his eyes suddenly like ice. 'I *expect* nothing, other than the pleasure of your company. I am no schoolboy ruled by the demands of my body, Portia.'

She shrugged, to mask the little chill that ran through her at the sudden coldness in his expressive voice. 'It's best to make things clear.'

Luc eyed her with hostility. 'Does this man of yours submit so tamely to such restrictions, Portia?'

'Not that it's any of your business, but as it happens he does.'

Luc shook his head in wonder. 'What kind of man is he?'

'A friend.'

'I was a fool to delude myself that *I* could be your friend.'

Portia was suddenly as angry as Luc. 'It's obvious

we'd better keep our acquaintance on a purely business level.'

'Which, of course, is what you value most.' The green eyes shot sparks of fire at her. 'As long as I buy Turret House it is all that matters to you, *n'est ce pas*?'

'It matters, yes.'

He looked at her in silence for a moment. 'As I said before, Portia, you are bad for my self-esteem.'

'Or possibly good for it,' she contradicted tartly. 'I suppose other women in your life fall over themselves to do whatever you want?'

Luc's eyebrows rose tauntingly. 'Are you curious about the women in my life?'

'Not in the least,' she lied.

'Then I shall not discuss them. I must go. I arranged an appointment for noon today.'

'Then I won't keep you,' said Portia tightly, and went ahead of him to the door. 'Goodbye, Luc. Thank you again for the roses.'

'I am glad you liked them,' he said, looking down at her broodingly. 'They reminded me of you.'

Her eyes narrowed. 'In what way?'

'Their tawny beauty—and their thorns.' He touched a finger to her unbruised cheek, and left without another word.

Not even an *au revoir*, she thought bitterly, and wondered who, exactly, he was on his way to meet.

Portia's eye had progressed to an angry plum colour ringed with green by next day, and, as expected, it provoked ribald, predictable comments from her male colleagues. Portia was in a bad mood by the time Biddy provided her with strong black coffee to kick-start her day.

'Are you telling the truth, Portia?' asked the middle-aged, streetwise Biddy. 'I mean, you didn't have a run-in with some bloke, by any chance?'

'No. I really did hit my head on a car window.' Portia thought for a moment. 'And if Monsieur Brissac—the man buying Turret House—rings, just take a message.'

'You mean whether you're here or not?' said Biddy sagely.

'Exactly.'

'Whatever you say. Mr Parrish wants a private word, by the way, when you've got a minute.'

When Portia went into Ben Parrish's office he rose and pulled out a chair. 'Take five and sit down.'

She did so, eyeing him questioningly. 'What's up?'

He looked away, shuffling papers in front of him on the desk. 'How much do you know about Luc Brissac?'

Startled by a secret leap of reaction, Portia shrugged casually. 'He's French, and represents a hotel chain. Other than that, not a lot.'

Ben eyed her uneasily. 'I feel a bit responsible because you had to get involved in the Turret House sale with him. It occurred to me you might like to know more about his background.'

Portia looked at him in alarm. 'Don't tell me he's not good for the money!'

Ben shook his head. 'Quite the reverse. Luc Brissac was only twenty-something when he turned the family château into a hotel, and just went on from there. His speciality is snapping up country houses and turning them into hotels—I quote—"famous for individuality and luxury". Both here and in France. The man's a millionaire.'

Portia stared at him. 'But he beat me down on the price of Turret House.'

'Of course he did. He's a businessman, Portia. He probably knew to the minute how long we'd had the place on our books.'

'So he meant to buy it right from the start,' she said, eyes kindling.

'I'd say, yes, he probably did.'

Portia sat burning with embarrassment as she remembered how Luc had not only conned her into a second visit to Turret House, but had demanded her life story before making a definite offer for the property. But *why*? What possible interest could a lowly estate agent have for someone wealthy enough to buy a hotel whenever he fancied one? She jumped to her feet, thanked Ben for the information, and assured him that the black eye wouldn't keep her from the day's appointments.

'Dark glasses and a hat, and no one will see,' she said brightly, and shut herself in her office, composing various flaying speeches to deliver when Luc rang.

But there was no call from Luc Brissac, that day or any other. Which infuriated Portia. She cringed as she thought of the kiss she'd volunteered. No wonder he'd expected her to fall into his arms. A man with his money could have any woman he wanted. Her eyes flashed. He'd soon find Portia Grant wasn't one of them.

Fortunately business was hotting up at Whitefriars. Spring was just around the corner, and with the appearance of the first daffodils enough demands for houses came in to keep all the partners busy full time. When Portia returned to the office mid-afternoon on the Friday Biddy was waiting, as usual, to take dictation for the letters and valuations she would send out the following Monday.

Biddy handed her a few messages she'd taken while Portia was out, but none of them was from Luc Brissac.

Which annoyed Portia so much she found it hard to concentrate on the job in hand. When the session was over she surprised herself, Biddy, and the rest of her colleagues, by announcing she was leaving early for once.

'Hot date?' said one of the senior partners, on his way in from a viewing.

'You bet. See you Monday.' Portia smiled at him and went out into the cold sunshine to make for the car park.

When she got home there was a message on her machine from Marianne.

'Hal's on call tonight. Fancy a film and supper afterwards? Ring me.'

The other message was from Joe. 'Fond hope, I suppose, but are you free tomorrow night? I thought we might try that new club I mentioned.'

Comforted to find herself in demand, Portia felt grateful to Joe for a Saturday night spent clubbing rather than alone, fuming over Luc Brissac. After an entire working week of expecting to hear from him every day, Portia felt let down, and disproportionately angry.

She admitted as much back at her flat, as she shared a pizza with Marianne after their return from the cinema.

'You like him, then?' asked her friend.

'Yes, I do.' Portia sighed glumly. 'But it's the usual story.'

'You mean he wants bed,' said Marianne bluntly. 'And you, of course, don't, as usual. Pity. Luc's not up to Hal's standard, of course, but he's eminently fanciable.'

'We hardly know each other.'

'What difference does that make? You can fall in love in the blink of an eye.'

Portia chuckled. 'You should know; you do it often enough.'

'Ouch! Put your claws away.' Marianne detached another segment of pizza thoughtfully. 'Actually, having met Hal, I realise I've never really been in love before. The others were just rehearsals. This is the real thing.'

Portia eyed her anxiously. This was something new. 'Does he mind about the others?' she asked. 'Or haven't you told him?'

'Oh, come on, love. I'm the same age as you. Of course he knows there were others. Do I look like a nun?' Marianne smiled philosophically. 'Besides, he's had relationships in the past, too. He knows perfectly well it's rare to get it right the first time.' She wagged her finger. 'And you weren't *always* so touch-me-not where men are concerned. When you were in college you had a boyfriend or two.'

'All right, all right,' said Portia irritably.

Marianne eyed her for a moment, then shrugged. 'I understand why you're wary of close relationships, love, but it's time you put all that behind you. In my opinion you should see something of the sexy Monsieur Brissac for a while.'

'Always supposing he wants to see me!' Portia shrugged. 'He hasn't rung me, so he's obviously lost interest.'

'And you mind?'

'Yes, I do.' With Marianne there was never any need to dissemble. 'But not in the way you think. I mind because he made a fool of me. He softened me up into selling Turret House for peanuts, when he's actually worth millions. He owns the wretched hotel chain, doesn't just represent it.'

'Golly!' said Marianne, impressed. 'All that Gallic charm and lots of dosh as well?'

'That's right.' Portia smiled brightly. 'Not that it mat-

ters. I'm going out with Joe tomorrow night. At least
with Joe what you see is what you get.'

'Hmm.'

'Joe's a great guy, Marianne, with exactly the same
ideas about fun as me. Which makes for an uncompli-
cated social life. So take that look off your face.'

'Sorry. It's just that I worry about you.'

'You needn't. Joe won't hurt me. If anyone's likely
to it's Luc Brissac—' Portia halted, biting her lip, and
Marianne nodded sagely.

'I told you. The blink of an eye.'

'I'm not in *love* with him. Just—attracted. Besides,
something about him makes me a bit uneasy.'

'What, exactly?'

'I wish I knew.' The phone rang, and Portia jumped
up to answer it, a tiny flicker of hope snuffed out as Hal
Courtney enquired about her head, then asked to speak
to Marianne.

Portia went off to the kitchen with the detritus of their
meal, and a moment later Marianne rushed in, starry-
eyed.

'Hal's picking me up here in a few minutes. Someone
else is taking over for him.'

Portia eyed her friend's translated face with wry
amusement. 'You're right. I've never seen you like this
before.'

Marianne gave her a mega-watt smile and hurried off
to the bathroom to do her face, as excited as a teenager.

When the buzzer ran Marianne catapulted to the door
to lift the receiver, and called, 'Come up,' then put it
back and gave her friend a hug. 'When shall I see you
again?'

'When Hal's on call again, I imagine,' said Portia
dryly.

They laughed together, then a knock on the door sent Marianne racing to fling it wide, her eagerness transformed to astonishment as she came face to face with Luc Brissac.

CHAPTER SIX

Luc smiled politely at Marianne, but his eyes were drawn to Portia's blank, unwelcoming face. 'Forgive me. I should have rung first, I know. But—'

The buzzer interrupted him, and Marianne kissed Portia, wished them both goodnight, and with a meaningful look over her shoulder at her friend hurried off to meet Hal.

'May I close the door?' enquired Luc, when it seemed unlikely Portia was ever going to say anything.

'Yes, of course.' She pulled herself together. 'This is a surprise.' And, because she was wearing jeans and a not very new sweater, topped by a shiny face and riotously untidy hair, she was furious.

'The surprise is not pleasant, I think,' he said, standing just inside the door. 'I apologise that it is so late.'

'Not at all,' said Portia formally. 'Come in. Do sit down. Can I offer you a drink, or coffee?'

'Nothing. Thank you.'

Portia sat down in her only armchair, and waved him to the sofa. Luc sat on the edge of it, looking tired, and not quite as elegant as usual. He had dark rings under his eyes and needed a shave, and instead of a formal suit he wore the familiar suede jacket with jeans and a blue chambray shirt.

'Your eye is better,' he said at last, when it seemed the silence would last indefinitely.

'Yes, thanks. How's the cut?'

'The stitch was removed, so it is better also.' He gave

her a look which clenched her stomach muscles beneath the denim. 'I am sorry I did not ring you.'

'No need for apologies. We're both busy people.'

'I was angry when I left you last week.'

'So I noticed.'

'I did not intend to return to London this weekend.' He breathed in deeply. 'But at last I came.'

'A business appointment?' she asked politely.

'You know I do not mean that,' he said with sudden violence. 'I came to see *you*, Portia. I could not keep away.'

She masked a leap of pleasure with cool indifference. 'If your idea was to spend time with me I'm flattered, of course, but you're out of luck. I'm tied up this weekend.'

His eyes blazed. 'With this *friend* of yours?'

'That's right,' she said evenly. 'With Joe.'

Luc jumped to his feet. 'Then of course I shall not trouble you further. May I ring for a taxi?'

'Of course.' Portia marched to the telephone, thrusting back her hair as she looked down the list of numbers for the cab-hire firm she sometimes used, her eyes blurred by a mist of angry tears.

Before she could dial the number a hand reached to take hers. Luc turned her towards him and held her wrists, his eyes burning down into hers.

'Portia, do not send me away without talking to me. For just a little while.'

'Are you sure you mean talk?' she said huskily, throwing down the gauntlet.

His jaw tightened. 'You look so irresistible tonight it would be a lie to say I do not want more than that. But if you wish me only to talk, and not to touch, then I shall obey. Are you not proud of taming me so, Portia?

I am not accustomed to—what do you say?—toe the line.'

'No. I can well believe that,' she snapped. 'So what do you want to talk about?'

He eyed her warily. 'I thought that friendship would be the perfect subject for discussion.'

'You mean you want that, after all?'

'No, I do not. If you demand the truth, then, yes. I desire more than that. But if it is the only thing possible between us—' He gave his expressive shrug.

'I do want the truth,' she said flatly.

'I just told you.'

'No, you haven't. I'm talking about money, Luc.'

He frowned. 'You mean you are dissatisfied with the price I paid for Turret House?'

'I'm not talking about Turret House,' she said with sudden heat, wrenching her hands away. 'At least, only indirectly. It's your devious approach I object to.'

'Devious?'

'Yes. Demanding details of my private life before you would clinch the deal. Did it amuse you to make a fool of me?' She flung away, but Luc caught her hand again, turning her to face him.

'Portia, you are angry with me, and I apologise. It was wrong of me to ask about your private life—'

'Particularly when you were so sparing with details of your own,' she said bitterly.

He dropped her hand, his face suddenly set in harsh, suspicious lines. 'What exactly do you mean?'

'You don't just represent the hotel chain, Monsieur Brissac, you own it. A pertinent little fact you withheld, no doubt, to make sure you got a good price for Turret House.'

Luc shrugged, obviously relieved. 'I gave no instructions at the Ravenswood to keep my background secret. And the price was the most I was prepared to pay for Turret House, whether you knew my financial standing or not.'

'Are you denying you implied that my confidences were part of the deal?' she demanded.

His lips tightened. 'No. I am not proud of that. But you are so poised and reserved, Portia. So British. I knew there was no other way of learning more about you in so short a time.'

'But *why* did you want to know?' she persisted.

He moved nearer, his eyes holding hers. 'You know why, *chérie*.'

'No, I don't,' said Portia, retreating.

'You lie. You know very well,' he said inexorably.

They stared at each other in tense, thickening silence, then the phone rang, breaking it, and Portia blinked owlishly, like someone waking from a heavy sleep.

She muttered an apology, and made for the phone, but before she reached it a hoarse voice began leaving a message.

'Hi, Portia, Joe here. I've come down with a filthy cold. I'm afraid tomorrow's off after all—' He broke off to cough. 'Sorry to mess you about. I'll call you as soon as I'm fit.'

'So. It seems you are free tomorrow after all,' said Luc, close behind her. 'Spend the day with me instead.'

She turned, meeting his eyes very squarely. 'I might have done if you'd rung me beforehand, as you promised. Probably you know dozens of women only too ready to drop everything and run when you crook your finger, Luc Brissac, but I'm different.'

'Ah, but I know that, Portia. It is this very difference which attracts me.' He smiled, spreading his hands. 'But if we do not spend time together how can we hope to be friends?'

Secretly conquered by the smile, Portia held out a moment or two longer, as though thinking it over, then inclined her head. 'All right, since I'm suddenly at a loose end, why not?'

This time Luc's smile was so victorious his triumph almost changed Portia's mind. But he was clever enough not to press home his advantage. 'It is almost possible for me to feel sorry for this man of yours, since he is ill.'

'I don't think you mean that.'

'I said "almost",' he reminded her.

Portia smiled. 'Have you eaten?'

'No, but do not disturb yourself.'

'It will not disturb me,' she mocked, 'to make you an omelette, Monsieur Brissac. If that will do?'

'It will be an honour! And so much more than I expected when I arrived,' he added soberly. 'At first I thought you would send me away without a word.'

'I probably would have done if Marianne hadn't been here.'

'Then I am grateful to your friend. I would send her flowers to express my gratitude, but I think the doctor would object.'

'I bet he would!' Portia led the way into her functional little kitchen. 'I don't have a dining table yet, so you'll have to eat here. Do sit down.'

'May I take off my jacket?' With a sigh of pleasure which disarmed Portia, he sat back in one of her kitchen chairs and asked about her day. Portia took out omelette pan and butter, and gathered a handful of herbs from the pots on her windowsill, describing the property sales she was involved in as she whisked eggs in a bowl. While the butter heated in the pan she cut slices from a rustic loaf, arranged slices of tomato on a bed of spinach leaves, and dressed them with oil and vinegar. Once the eggs hissed in the hot butter it was only a minute or so before a perfect omelette was set in front of her guest.

'So you can cook also,' he stated indistinctly through the first mouthful.

'Also?' she queried, taking the other chair.

Luc helped himself to the salad. 'You are clever, beautiful, successful.' He smiled at her. 'Career women are not always good cooks.'

'My mother taught me to cook when I was young.' She sobered, and Luc reached out a hand to touch hers.

'Now I have made you sad.'

She shook her head, smiling. 'Not really.'

'Good.' He ate the rest of his meal with flattering relish, and at last sat back with a sigh. 'That was perfect. Sometimes the most basic, simple things in life are the best.'

'But it's nice to splash out on a bit of luxury now and then. I enjoyed the caviare and lobster at the hotel.' She raised an eyebrow at him and she took his plate. 'Though I didn't know then that I had the owner himself to thank for it.'

Luc stretched out his long legs and sat with his hands clasped behind his head, watching her with open pleasure as she restored the kitchen to order. 'When did you learn the truth, Portia?'

'Last Monday. Ben Parrish took it on himself to enlighten me.'

'To reassure you I was good for the money for Turret House?'

'That too, knowing Ben.' Portia turned to face him.

'But he also thought I might be interested in your background.'

'And you were angry when he told you, of course?' said Luc, resigned.

'Yes. Not that I had any right to be. I don't usually demand personal details from my clients.' She filled the kettle. 'Coffee?'

'Thank you. Yes.' He frowned. 'Why were you angry?'

Portia looked at him squarely. 'If we do become friends from now on—'

'As we will!' he assured her.

'How can you be sure it wasn't your money which changed my mind?'

'I am sure,' he said, with utter certainty. 'I was not always wealthy. *Vraiment*, there was a time when I had very little ready money at all. But...' He hesitated, a wry smile twisting his mouth.

She nodded, resigned. 'Your success with my sex has never depended on money.'

'Exactly,' he said simply.

Portia gave him a crooked little smile. 'Not much wrong with your self-esteem tonight!' She handed him a cup of coffee. 'Let's sit in the other room.'

Portia curled up in her chair and Luc sat down on her sofa, looking utterly relaxed.

'This,' he said, 'is worth all the trouble.'

'Trouble?'

He nodded. 'There was a late crisis at my Paris office. I barely had time to change before driving to the airport, only to find my flight was delayed. When I arrived in London I told myself to be patient, to wait until tomorrow to see you, but—' He shrugged, his eyes on hers.

'Since meeting you I am regressed to boyhood. I was impatient. I could not wait until then.'

Portia's heart skipped a beat. 'If you'd arrived earlier I wouldn't have been here. I went to the cinema with Marianne.'

'Then I would have waited until you arrived,' he assured her.

She stared at him, startled, and realised he meant it. 'Then now you are here, and I've agreed to spend the day with you tomorrow, what would you like to do?'

Luc leaned forward, his hands clasped loosely between his knees. 'You choose, Portia. This is your city. Lunch, of course, then perhaps a trip up the Thames, or a theatre matinée? If you were alone, what would you do?'

'I tend to be very lazy on winter weekends,' she admitted. 'At this time of year I generally hire a video or two, read a lot, go shopping sometimes.'

'That sounds good. With you I would enjoy such things very much.' He eyed her searchingly. 'If I suggest lunch in my apartment will you suspect me of dark and devious motives again, Portia?'

She looked at him levelly. 'And will you lose your temper and get very brooding and French if I say I'd rather not?'

He sat very still. 'Are you saying,' he began with care, 'that you have changed your mind?'

'No. I'd simply prefer to keep to my home ground for a while.'

Luc relaxed slightly. 'Whatever you wish, Portia. So, what shall we do tomorrow? Sunday, also,' he added firmly.

'When do you go back to Paris?' she asked, making

no attempt to lie about some fictitious Sunday engagement.

'Early Monday morning. Until then I want to spend as much time with you as possible. And,' he added, leaning forward to emphasise the point, 'I talk of the days only. I am not demanding your company in my bed. You see? I, too, am learning caution.'

Portia smiled. 'Something new for you?'

He shook his head. 'In matters of business I am never precipitate. In affairs of the emotions, of course, it is different.'

'Have you been in love very often, then?' she asked curiously.

A smile played at a corner of the wide, sensuous mouth. 'Of course. When I was young I was never *out* of love.' He sobered. 'Then my father died suddenly and my carefree days were over.'

'Something like me.'

He shook his head. 'I was more fortunate than you, *chérie*. With my mother's aid I at least found a way to keep Beau Rivage.'

'Your home? Ben told me you turned it into a hotel.'

'He was right. My mother sold some paintings, which aided the original changes, and from the first the venture was a success.' He shrugged. 'But there was no time any more for falling in—and out—of love, Portia.'

'You were too busy saving your inheritance?'

'Not solely mine,' he informed her. 'The estate was left to the entire family. But the others were young, so the responsibility was mine.'

'That must have been hard for you,' said Portia, fascinated by this glimpse into the Brissac past. 'Had your house been in the family a long time?'

'No. I was born in Paris. But my mother is Bretonne

from St Malo, so my father bought Beau Rivage for her about twenty years ago, with the intention of restoring it to its former glories. It was built in the early eighteenth century, and is changed remarkably little. My father regarded it as his life work. Unfortunately his life was cut short.'

'Had he completed all the restoration?'

'Most of it, yes. But the only way to conserve it was to make it pay for itself. The location of Beau Rivage is ideal for a hotel. From the first it became popular with tourists, many of them your countrymen from across La Manche.'

'You mean the English Channel,' she said, laughing.

'Another difference! Tell me, Portia, are such differences obstacles to friendship between us?'

'Why should they be?' She paused. 'Or are there any more dark secrets I should know, Luc?'

He was silent for a moment, then looked up to meet her eyes. 'I am not married, nor do I possess a fiancée. I own an apartment in Paris, another in London, and I visit Beau Rivage to see my mother regularly. It is no longer a hotel. Once the chain was established and successful this was no longer necessary. My sisters are married, so my mother lives there alone.' His eyes darkened, and Portia felt a pang of sympathy for the father who had died, like her own, too young. 'But my sisters visit Beau Rivage with their children, so my mother is rarely alone for long there.'

There was silence in the room for a while, and Luc's eyes focused inwards, as though remembering times past.

Portia got up and collected the coffee cups. 'Would you like a drink, Luc, or are you driving back to your flat?'

'No, I came by taxi. Is it possible to get one at this time of night?'

'As long as you're not in a rush, yes.'

'I am in no rush at all,' he assured her, and smiled. 'But I do not wish to outstay my welcome.'

'I didn't give you much of a welcome when you arrived,' said Portia wryly.

'No,' he agreed, and looked at her challengingly. 'You feel warmer towards me now?'

'A bit,' she admitted, and smiled. 'I'll sort out a taxi for you, then the choice of beverage is tea, coffee, some of your French designer water, or a glass of wine I doubt very much will come up to your standards. Joe brought it last time he was here.'

'Then I will not drink it,' said Luc instantly, and rose to his feet. 'If you will ring for the taxi, Portia, all I want until it arrives is to talk to you.' The look in his eyes took her breath away. 'Do not waste time in making coffee. Just sit with me for a while. Please?'

'All right,' she said unevenly, and went over to the telephone to ring the company she normally used, to be told it would be forty minutes or so before a cab was free.

'So,' said Luc, standing in the middle of the room where she'd left him. 'I am granted forty minutes more of your company.'

'That's just tonight,' she pointed out.

He moved closer and put out a finger to touch her cheekbone. 'The bruise is almost gone, or are you using some clever *maquillage*?'

'I don't have any make-up on at all,' she retorted. 'Which was one of the reasons I wasn't very welcoming when you turned up tonight.'

'But why?' he said, mystified.

'You're always so elegant. I was furious at being caught with a shiny face and my hair all over the place, not to mention these clothes—'

'But you are so appealing like this. So much more approachable than the businesslike Miss Grant with the severe *coiffure* and tailored suits.' He caught her hand and drew her down on the sofa beside him. 'And tonight I am not elegant at all. My clothes are just like yours, and I am very conscious that I need a shave.'

She grinned at him. 'We're just a couple of scruffs, in fact!'

'Scruffs?'

She explained, laughing, and he chuckled with her, then stretched out his legs with a sigh, and turned his head on the sofa-back to look at her.

'It is so good to be with you like this tonight. My week was disaster from the time I left you until now.'

'Why?'

'Turret House is not my only concern at present. I am negotiating the purchase of a small château in Provence.'

'What's it like?' asked Portia, curling up beside him.

'Very Provençal, with gold sandstone towers and wood shutters, and great bronze urns full of flowers on the terrace.'

'Sounds wonderful,' she said, with a sigh.

'If I buy it I will take you there,' he said softly, his eyes moving over her face to catch every nuance of the reaction she was determined to hide.

'So why the disaster?' she asked matter-of-factly. 'Are the owners reluctant to sell?'

'Their price is unrealistic, because the property is not in good repair. And, at the moment, my offer is too low for the lady who owns it.' He shrugged philosophically.

'But in the end, as always, there will be a compromise. and then the château will be mine.'

'And what will the lady do then?'

'Do not feel pity for her, *chérie*. She is anxious to retire to her apartment in Nice—and live very well on the money I shall pay her.'

'You do a great deal of research, I suppose, before you begin negotiations?'

'But of course. My lawyers have an office in Nice. Also I employ staff who—very discreetly, of course— stay in the area for a while, and find out as much as possible about the property I am interested in.' He slid his arm along the back of the sofa, not quite touching her shoulders. 'Do you disapprove of my business tactics?'

'Of course not.' She turned her head to smile at him. 'I'm in the same line of business myself, remember.'

'For which I am most thankful. Otherwise, Mademoiselle Grant, I might never have met you.' His eyes grew suddenly intent and dropped to her mouth, and, suddenly flustered, Portia said the first thing that came into her head.

'Is your mouth better?' she asked, then blushed vividly, certain he would take it as a blatant invitation.

'Your kiss would complete the cure,' he said huskily, then let out a long, unsteady breath and drew her very slowly into his arms. When she made no objection he pulled her close with one arm, his free hand threading through the tumbled curls as he brought her face up to his. For a long, searching moment he looked deep into her eyes, then at last laid his mouth on hers.

With Marianne's words ringing in her ears, Portia offered no resistance. Nor wanted to. Her lips opened to the seeking, skilled mouth, and her arm went up to encircle his neck, a tremor running through her as his tongue found hers and caressed it with slow, savouring delight at her response. Luc's breathing grew faster, his kisses gradually fiercer, then hungry with demand, until at last he tore his lips from hers to gasp incoherent French endearments as he buried his face in her hair.

The buzzer on Portia's door brought them both to their feet, and she hurried to pick up the receiver while Luc collected his jacket from the kitchen.

'Your cab,' she said breathlessly, pushing her hair back behind her ears.

Luc touched a hand to her chin, his eyes rueful. 'Last time I left you with a black eye. This time I have made your skin red, *chérie*.'

'It didn't hurt—or if it did I didn't notice it,' she assured him, smiling, and with a smothered sound he pulled her back into his arms and kissed her fiercely. 'Now I must go,' he said unevenly, and put her from him. 'Perhaps it is just as well the taxi arrived when it did. I will return early in the morning.'

'Not too early. I need a bit of a shop at the supermarket.'

'I shall drive you there,' he said promptly. 'Very carefully this time.'

'That's a relief,' she said, grinning. 'But if you don't go soon the cab will give up and take off without you.'

'If it did, would you let me stay?' he demanded.

'Certainly not.' She smiled to soften the refusal. 'Goodnight, Luc.'

He touched a hand to her cheek. 'Until tomorrow, Portia.'

CHAPTER SEVEN

NORMALLY Portia allowed herself extra time in bed in the morning on free weekends, but this particular Saturday she was up at first light to wash her hair and shower and give herself time to search in her wardrobe for something which would look effortlessly perfect for the occasion.

When she was finally ready for whatever the day promised, in cinnamon velvet jeans and creamy cashmere sweater, Portia ran a brush through crackling waves and curls and left them loose on her shoulders. And, because Luc had professed himself enchanted with her unadorned face the night before, she spent a shamelessly long time in applying various subtle aids to look as though she'd used no cosmetics at all. She was drinking her first coffee of the day when her bell rang.

Sure it couldn't be Luc at just gone nine she picked up the receiver and flushed with pleasure when a familiar, husky voice said, '*Bonjour*, Portia. Am I too early?'

'No. Come up.' When he knocked a little later she threw open the door, smiling in welcome.

Luc promptly dropped a large paper bag on the floor and took her in his arms, kissing her on both cheeks.

'That is a much better welcome than last night,' he said in approval, and handed her the bag, which was warm and gave out mouthwatering scents of hot pastry. 'Croissants,' he said, and sniffed the air. 'Do I smell coffee?'

'Yes. Just made it.' Portia chuckled. 'When you said the entire day you really meant it, then?'

'But of course!'

Portia normally disliked breakfast of any kind other than a cup of tea or coffee. This particular, surprising morning she found she was hungry, as she shared the croissants with Luc and made a second pot of coffee. 'I wouldn't have put you down as domesticated,' she commented, as he filled their cups for the third time.

'I am very useful in the kitchen,' he assured her smugly. 'If you like I will make dinner for you. This morning we shall go shopping for food, and afterwards we will eat lunch somewhere, then tonight, before we watch these videos of yours, I shall impress you with my skill as chef.'

Portia regarded him in amusement over her coffee cup. Luc was informal, but no less elegant than usual, in dark needlecord trousers, his wool shirt creamy white against his smooth olive skin and thick black hair. His eyes narrowed in response to her smile.

'You are laughing at me?'

'It's hard to believe you've ever cooked anything in your life.'

He shook his head. 'I was not always wealthy, Portia. Also my mother is a formidable cook, and insisted that all her children should be capable of creating one or two simple dishes at the very least. You and I share that in common, *n'est ce pas*?' He gave her a long, green look. 'I believe that as our friendship progresses we shall discover many more things in common.'

'It's possible,' she admitted cautiously.

'It is certain,' he contradicted. 'Where is your dishwasher?'

Portia chuckled, and held up her hands. 'These wash my dishes.'

Luc leaned across the table and seized them, planting a kiss in each palm. 'Not today,' he said firmly.

It was strangely sweet to Portia to dry dishes as Luc washed them, a chore never undertaken in this particular kitchen by any man. In her flat-sharing days some of the unwilling male tenants had sometimes been bullied into a few chores, but though Joe sometimes came back to the flat for coffee, or a nightcap, he'd never suggested setting foot in Portia's kitchen, nor had she wanted him to. The present situation was doubly welcome, because before Luc arrived Portia had worried that he might expect to take up where he'd left off, after the passionate leave-taking of the night before. Instead his exuberant greeting had been more affectionate than passionate. And reassuring, just like his insistence on washing dishes. As, she thought with sudden intuition, he'd meant it all to be.

'Those beautiful dark eyes look thoughtful,' observed Luc as he dried his hands. 'Is the price in England still one penny for such thoughts?'

'Not in this case,' she assured him. 'Mine are not for sale.'

'Perhaps one day you will give me all your private thoughts freely,' said Luc, and touched a hand to her cheek. '*Alors*, let us get on with the shopping. Do we drive far?'

'No. Nor, thank goodness, do we go on a motorway,' she teased.

Shopping with Luc was fun, other than his tendency towards extravagance which Portia tried in vain to curb.

'No, I don't want smoked salmon, nor truffle oil. I need things like breakfast cereal, and coffee.'

Ignoring her protests, Luc began filling her trolley with all kinds of delicacies, including a bottle of champagne, leaving Portia to add more prosaic staples. When they arrived at the checkout he paid before she could prevent him.

'You shouldn't have done that,' she scolded, as he loaded the car. 'We'll settle up when we get to the flat.'

Luc merely laughed at her, patting her cheek. 'Such an independent lady. Last week I bought you roses; this week I buy you groceries. What difference does it make?'

'And before that you paid for my room, dinner, lunch, provided a picnic—'

'And last night you made me an omelette. Should I have refused because I did not pay for the eggs?'

'That's sophistry,' she said, laughing, as he drove off.

'You talk as though I offer you a mink coat—'

'Bad move all round. Real fur's frowned on these days.'

'Do not change the subject,' he said severely. 'So listen, Portia, because I am going to be very, very blunt now you are captive in the car.'

She eyed him uneasily. 'What do you mean?'

Luc kept his eyes on the road. 'To buy you roses, or pay for a meal, gives me pleasure. But these are not the dark and devious motives you suspect. I know that the only way to become your lover is for you to want that as much as I do. If this is never possible for you I will just be your friend, and perhaps kiss you now and then, because to be in your company for long and not kiss you at all is an impossibility for me, you understand. So, if

you do not permit even this please say so now while I
still—' He stopped.

'While you still what?' she prompted.

'While I still possess the strength to say goodbye.'

Neither of them said any more until they reached her
flat.

'So?' said Luc at last. He leaned in the doorway, arms
folded, watching her neat, methodical movements as
Portia put the food away.

She frowned at him fleetingly, then resumed her task.
'Are you giving me an ultimatum, Luc?'

'No. I am striving to be honest.' He looked at her
steadily. 'Are you willing for a loving friendship? Or for
you must the friendship be purely platonic?'

From the first moment he'd kissed her in Turret House
Portia had known very well that a platonic relationship
with Luc Brissac was impossible. But one thing became
clearer with each moment she spent in his company. She
wanted *some* kind of relationship with him. If he said
goodbye and walked out right now she'd regret it, she
knew with certainty. She turned to face the green as-
sessing scrutiny.

'I don't want you to say goodbye, Luc.' Which was
as near as she would ever get to the answer he wanted.

'Good. I do not want it either,' he assured her. 'So let
us find a place to eat.'

'Right,' she said, suddenly practical. 'I know a nice,
unpretentious little wine bar where they serve a couple
of French dishes every day. The wine's not bad either.
Are you game?'

'Game?'

'Willing, then.'

He brushed a hand over her hair and smiled down into

her eyes. 'I am willing to do anything you wish, Portia. Always.'

Later, with plates of warm tuna flan in front of them, Luc nodded in surprised approval as he tasted his. 'It was clever of you to find a place with Breton cuisine.'

'I didn't know it was Breton,' she confessed. 'This is gorgeous, though. I wonder what's in this sauce?'

Luc tasted it, eyes concentrated. 'Lemon juice, herbs, and crème fraîche, I think. It goes well with this particular fish. The giant tuna has been the goal of Breton fishermen since the Middle Ages.'

They lingered over coffee afterwards, relaxed in each other's company, talking without pause. And afterwards they raced from the car into Portia's building through pouring, sleet-filled rain, gasping for breath as the lift took them up to her flat.

'And now,' said Luc, as they took off wet coats, 'I must ask you a favour. Even though,' he added sombrely, 'it may put a great strain on our friendship.'

'Oh, yes?' said Portia, eyes narrowed. 'What is it?'

'I would very much like to watch television. France is playing England at Twickenham this afternoon. Do you dislike rugby, Portia?'

'No. I'm an ardent rugby fan, I'd have you know.' She smiled at him. 'In college I had friends who played in the first fifteen.'

'Of course you did,' he said, resigned, then his eyes lit with an unholy gleam. 'Let us make a bet. If France wins you will pay me two kisses.'

'Done,' she said promptly. 'What happens if England wins? As they will, of course.'

'Fighting talk, *mademoiselle*. For which I shall pay you one kiss.'

'Why do I have to pay you more than you pay me, Luc Brissac?'

'Because,' he said patiently, as though explaining to a child, 'I want your kisses more than you want mine.'

Portia flushed, and took his coat. 'I'll put this to dry.'

He smiled at her indulgently, and switched on the television. 'Hurry, Portia, it is nearly time for the kick-off.'

She hung their wet coats in the airing cupboard, then went into the kitchen, needing a moment to herself. Luc was wrong. She wanted his kisses every bit as much as he wanted hers. And, if she were brutally honest, kissing was just a euphemism for what both of them really wanted. But though her body urged her to say yes to anything Luc desired, her reason advised caution. Three weeks ago neither of them had known of each other's existence.

A sudden roar from her sitting room sent Portia hurrying in to join Luc. 'What's happened?'

'We scored in the first five minutes!' he informed her jubilantly. 'Come, Portia, your team needs your encouragement,' he added gloatingly.

She laughed and sat down beside him, then wished she hadn't, since Luc jumped up every time France took the game forward, and when they scored a second time raised the roof with his shout of triumph.

Then England fought back, and it was Portia's turn for jubilation. By half-time the scores were level, and in the interval she hotly debated every aspect of the game with Luc. When the match resumed there was no let-up in the excitement, which mounted with every minute until the French backs surged away in a brilliant passing move across the field, culminating in a rocket-like burst of speed by the full-back as he eluded clutching English hands to ground the ball behind the posts for France.

'Formidable!' roared Luc, punching the air with his fist as the outside-half converted the try with a ball sent over the crossbar, plumb between the uprights.

'There's time yet,' said Portia loyally, her faith rewarded when England equalised with only a minute or two to go. Then, just as it seemed certain the game would end, unusually, in a draw, the French outside-half sent the ball sailing between the posts for a textbook drop-kick, and won the game for France.

Luc cheered wildly, then turned to seize Portia by the elbows. 'So,' he said, eyes glittering, 'you owe me two kisses, *mademoiselle.*'

'So I do.' She eyed him challengingly. 'Want them now?'

'He shook his head. 'I will save your kisses until we say goodnight. Otherwise—' He released her abruptly. 'If I start kissing you now, Portia, I might not want to stop.'

Portia got up, secretly rather disappointed. 'Right,' she said briskly. 'Time for tea.'

He raised an eyebrow. 'Tea?'

'You can drink coffee, if you like,' she said, laughing.

But Luc gallantly drank tea, and ate more than his share of the scones and clotted cream Portia had brought from the supermarket, all the time discussing the game and how good it had been. Portia entered into the discussion with passion, defending her team with a ferocity which Luc very obviously found enchanting.

'Mon Dieu,' he said at last. 'If this is how you are when you lose, you must be unbearable in victory, Portia.'

'Sorry,' she said, laughing. 'I tend to get over enthusiastic.'

'Ah, yes. The rugby-playing boyfriends!'

'Did you play rugby?'

'As a boy, only. Later I had no time. Now, Portia,' he added, 'what is next on the programme?'

Portia drew the curtains against the darkening afternoon. 'I suggest we watch one of the videos until it's time for dinner.'

Luc watched as she put the film in the VCR, then held out his hand. 'Come and sit beside me, Portia.'

The film was a fast-moving comedy, and they laughed together, enjoying the film almost as much as each other's company. And afterwards Portia teased Luc unmercifully about his skill at cooking when she found this consisted mainly of arranging a platter with ham, salami and pâté, and several kinds of cheese, his only real creation a colourful salad and the dressing to go with it.

'Tonight, because it is the first time we do this together, I consider time spent over an elaborate dish as time wasted, *chérie*.' He looked at her. 'If you were alone tonight, what would you eat?'

'Something very like this,' she admitted, 'on a smaller scale.'

'Then to make this meal special we shall drink champagne,' he insisted, and took the bottle from her fridge. He removed the cork with a deft thrust of his thumbs, and filled the glasses she gave him. 'A toast.'

She raised her glass, smiling. 'What shall we drink to?'

Luc touched her glass with his. 'To us, Portia.'

'To us,' she echoed, and tasted the wine with respect, and a certain amount of caution. Luc Brissac and vintage champagne were a heady combination. She would do well to tread warily.

'What is going on behind those beautiful dark eyes?' asked Luc, helping her to salad.

'I was thinking how very pleasant this is,' she said, with complete truth.

'If you were with this man—'

'His name is Joe. Joe Marcus.'

'*Bien.* What would you be doing?'

'He suggested a new club he'd heard about.'

'You would like this club?'

'I don't know, I've never been there.'

Luc shook his head reprovingly. 'You know exactly what I mean, Portia. For me, an evening here with you like this is a delight, but if your preference was a nightclub I would have been most pleased to escort you.'

Portia went on with her meal in silence for a moment. Unknown to Luc, she infinitely preferred being alone with him in complete privacy rather than in some crowded club, however fashionable. 'I've had a busy week. I'm rather glad to stay home.'

He reached a hand across the table and touched hers fleetingly. 'So am I. It has been a good day. Not,' he added, 'that it is over yet. There is still the other film to watch. It is about murder, you said. Do you frighten easily?'

She smiled at him. 'If I do you can hold my hand.'

Luc's eyes darkened, and he seemed on the point of saying something, then shrugged and pressed her to more ham, leaving Portia curious about the words he'd left unsaid.

Later Luc insisted on switching out all but one lamp, to aid atmosphere, and sat close beside Portia on the sofa. When she gave a gasp at a particularly scary scene, instead of taking her hand Luc put his arm round her and kept it there until the end of the film. By the time the credits rolled both of them were tense and silent, and the moment Portia aimed the remote control at the screen

Luc drew her back into his arms and turned her face up
to his.

'I want the kisses now, *chérie*,' he said huskily, taking
possession of her mouth with a ragged sigh of pleasure
at the contact. His lips moved over hers, coaxing them
open, and she shivered a little as his tongue began to
follow the same path over her parted lips, then slid between them, his mouth gradually more persuasive as he
sought her response. Startled by the leap of fire in her
blood, Portia gasped, and Luc crushed her close, his
mouth fierce with demand she responded to so utterly
that he tore his lips from hers at last and thrust a hand
into her hair, holding her still as he looked down into
her eyes with such heat her mouth dried.

'This is not easy, Portia,' he said harshly.

She stared at him, dazed. 'Does your lip hurt?'

'It is not my lip that troubles me! You are irresistible,
ma belle. It is impossible just to kiss and want no more
than that.' He smiled down at her crookedly. 'I am not
made of stone, Portia.'

'Neither am I,' she said deliberately, and felt secret
muscles clench as his eyes blazed his response.

Very slowly, his eyes looking deep into hers, he drew
a hand down her cheek, then followed its progress with
his lips, kissing her throat as he stroked the outline of
her breasts through the soft cashmere. Portia stirred restlessly, unable to sit still under his touch, and Luc, in
tune with every nuance of her response, slid his hands
under the thin wool, caressing her satin-covered breasts
with a delicacy so erotic Portia began to breathe shal-
lowly, uttering a hoarse little sound he smothered with
his kiss as his hands slid behind her to release the catch
and her breasts surged, bare and taut, into his waiting
hands.

Luc buried his face in her hair as his thumbs moved in soft, abrasive caresses over her nipples, causing such tumult inside Portia that she sat up suddenly and held up her arms. Luc drew a rasping breath and slid the sweater over her head. He tossed the scrap of satin aside, then gazed at her with a molten look so tactile she felt it on her skin as it roved over her in slow, pulse-quickening relish. Her nipples hardened, and her breath suddenly laboured in her chest as she thrust herself against him and buried her face against his shoulder, unable to endure his gaze a moment longer.

'Mon Dieu,' he said hoarsely. 'You are so beautiful, so alluring. Can you understand how you make me feel?' He held her closer, his breath catching in his throat as her breasts flattened against his chest.

Portia shook her head. 'Not like this,' she said gruffly, and began to undo his shirt. But he tore it open, sending buttons flying in all directions in his impatience to feel her naked breasts against his chest. Luc buried his face in her tangled curls, uttering a torrent of husky, erotic French into her uncomprehending ear as his hands moved restlessly over her bare back.

At last she pushed him away a little, smiling shakily into his smouldering eyes. 'In school my French teacher never used words like that,' she whispered.

'Then I must teach you the language of love, ma belle.' Luc bent his head, his hair brushing her skin as he kissed the slopes of her breasts, his tongue tasting the satiny curves. Then he took one of the quivering, diamond-hard tips between his lips, his teeth grazing delicately on the sensitised flesh, and Portia gasped as darts of fire found their target deep inside her. Her head went back, threshing from side to side as Luc played clever havoc with lips and teeth and fingertips, until her entire body was blazing with need. For a long, timeless interval Luc made love to her with relentless skill, until his own artistry finally defeated him.

Abruptly he jumped up and put his shirt back on, his eyes averted. 'If I take even one look at you, I am lost,' he panted. 'Have mercy, Portia. Cover yourself before I lose my head completely.'

Dazed, surprised, and utterly frustrated, Portia pulled on her sweater with trembling, uncoordinated fingers.

'I'm respectable again,' she told him, and Luc thrust his shirt inside his belt and turned to look down at her, his jaw set.

'I did not realise I possessed such strength of mind,' he said bitterly. 'To let you go just then was not easy, Portia.'

She drew in a deep, shaky breath. 'Then why did you?'

Luc sat down beside her, leaving a space between them as he took her hand in his, his eyes holding hers as he smoothed her skin with a caressing finger. 'Because I was afraid that if I followed my desire to its natural conclusion you would think this was my sole reason for coming here this weekend.'

A faint smile played at the corners of her mouth. 'But, as you told me before, Monsieur Brissac, if a sexual encounter was all you had in mind you could have achieved that in Paris and saved yourself the price of an airfare.' She looked at him levelly. 'Unless, of course, you are combining business with pleasure this weekend.'

'Of course I am,' he said promptly. 'I am a client spending time with a partner of Whitefriars Estates to clinch the sale of Turret House.' He laid a caressing fingertip on her bottom lip. 'That not one word about business shall pass our lips this weekend will be our little secret, *chérie.*'

'One I'll keep to myself, too,' she said with feeling.

'Do not look at me like that, *ma belle*, or your client's good intentions will vanish,' he advised hoarsely, and moved farther away. 'Perhaps I should leave now, while I can.'

'It's early yet,' she said quickly.

Luc's eyes glittered. 'You know very well I am delighted that you wish me to stay, Portia. But I warn you that you must keep your distance. I have no defence against your touch.'

'Then I won't touch you,' she assured him, and curled up in the safety of the armchair.

Luc smiled ruefully, and asked about the programme for next day. 'For myself, I would like nothing better than another day spent like this one,' he said, from the far corner of the sofa.

'Fine by me,' she assured him. 'Heaven knows we bought enough food today.'

'I would like to make one change, Portia.' Luc gave her a long, steady look. 'Now you can trust my self-control, will you come to my apartment tomorrow?'

'Yes,' she said without hesitation.

He eyed her in surprise. 'You know, Portia, I did not expect you to agree so quickly.'

'I'm curious to see your flat,' she said candidly. 'Besides, I've enjoyed today. All of it.'

Luc breathed in deeply. 'I, too, *chérie*. So come early tomorrow.'

CHAPTER EIGHT

Luc Brissac's London base was a first-floor flat in a large, handsome house built at the turn of the century. When he conducted her through it the following morning, early, as he'd insisted, Portia was deeply impressed by the large rooms and floor-to-ceiling arched windows, and envied him the conservatory he used as an office. The entire flat gave an instant impression of light and space, even on a cold February morning.

'This is lovely,' said Portia, her cheeks glowing from the kisses Luc had planted on them when she arrived. 'Is it all your own taste?'

'It is to my taste, but only the furniture is mine. The decor is the work of the interior designer who sold the flat to me—through your agency, of course.' He smiled at her appreciatively. 'You look very beautiful this morning, Portia.'

Since she'd been up at first light expending much effort on her appearance she was glad he thought so. 'Thank you,' she said demurely. 'You look pretty good yourself.'

'If I do,' he said, with a bow, 'it is because I spent such a perfect day yesterday.'

'So did I,' she said candidly. 'Now, where's this breakfast you promised me?'

The day proved no less perfect than the one before as they ate brioche and coffee at Luc's dining table, then went for a walk on Hampstead Heath to sharpen an appetite for lunch in a restaurant where Luc was obviously well known.

'Do you come here often to Sunday lunch?' she asked.

He smiled indulgently. 'Very rarely, Portia. Normally I do not spend my weekends in London. My business visits to Britain are made during the week. I dine here occasionally, but this is the first time for Sunday lunch.'

'Then why did you stipulate a weekend for the viewing at Turret House?' she asked, frowning.

'It was the only time I had free at that point. 'Ah, good,' he added as a waiter approached. 'Here is our meal.'

The pie he had suggested they share was filled with monkfish and bacon, flavoured with thyme and vermouth and topped with a featherlight crust, and it tasted sublime, Portia assured him.

'I like to see a woman eat,' said Luc with satisfaction, then frowned. 'Do you eat well during the week, Portia?'

'Not like this! Lunch is usually a sandwich, and dinner something simple. 'I eat a lot of soup in winter.'

He eyed her disapprovingly. 'It is plain I must come to London every weekend in future, to make sure you eat enough to last through the week. This does not meet with your approval?' he demanded, at the look on her face.

'*Every* weekend?' she asked quietly.

Luc put down his knife and fork and leaned forward, looking at her steadily. 'Perhaps I should have said every weekend that you consent to spare me.' He smiled. 'Now, you must eat dessert, Portia, Or pudding, as you Brits say. I insist.'

When he refused to take no for an answer she eventually consented to share the cheese he chose, and it was well into the afternoon by the time the meal was over.

'We shall drink coffee at the apartment, and maybe a cognac,' he suggested, as he drove her back. 'I propose we dine at home tonight, Portia.'

She blew our her cheeks. 'Luc, I won't be able to—'

'You mean you must leave early?' he said, frowning.

'No. I *meant* that after the lunch we've just eaten I won't be able to eat again until breakfast tomorrow.'

He gave her a sidelong glance that brought colour rushing to her face. 'I would very much like you to stay with me until then, *chérie*—but do not flash your eyes at me. I know very well you will say no.' He smiled straight ahead through the windscreen. 'I suppose I must content myself with the memory of the two breakfasts shared with you already.'

When they got back to Luc's flat neither of them felt energetic enough to do anything more demanding than talk as they idled away the rest of the afternoon together, until at last Portia was feeling distinctly drowsy.

'I'm sorry,' she said with contrition, after a second stifled yawn. 'It must be the lunch, and the warmth in here.'

'Also I insisted you came so early this morning,' said Luc, and swung her feet up on the chesterfield sofa they were sharing. He put cushions behind her head, then drew his finger down her cheek. 'I must work for a while, so sleep, *chérie*.'

When Portia woke the room was in semi-darkness, the only light the glow from the conservatory. At some point Luc had covered her with a light rug, and she lay quietly, feeling warm and relaxed and utterly disinclined to move. She would stay like this for a little while, she decided. Until Luc had finished what he was doing...

She woke the second time to find Luc lying full-length beside her, his eyes only inches from hers in the half-

light. He smiled, and she smiled back, and he tossed the
rug away and took her in his arms.

'This seems a little dangerous,' she said huskily, as
his proximity made it very obvious that he wanted her.

'Dangerous?' he queried in amusement, the faint trace
of accent causing a familiar tightening of muscles in that
part of Portia in close contact with the corresponding
part of Luc. 'You are in no danger, Portia. My intention
was to wake you with a kiss, but you were so beautiful
lying there I could not resist joining you instead.'

Portia lay silent and still in his possessive embrace for
a long interval, very much aware that she was Luc's
captive. One part of her was outraged to find she liked
it. But another part, the one that had begun to get out of
hand ever since her first meeting with him, gave instructions her body was all too willing to obey. Her hips
thrust closer against his and her lips parted, her eyes
lambent with invitation. Answering heat flared in Luc's,
and he began to breathe more rapidly. Portia's heart
thudded against his chest, and he inhaled sharply, his
jaw tightening until she could see the muscles taut in his
neck. She moved the fraction nearer that brought her
mouth in contact with his throat, and Luc gave an ex-
plosive sigh and tipped her face up to his.

To her surprise he didn't kiss her senseless, as she
wanted, but slid his hand into her hair to hold her face
far enough away for his eyes to look deep into hers.

'You were right, Portia,' he said harshly. 'This is very
dangerous. It will take only one kiss to light a fire impossible to control.'

It was a prospect which took Portia's breath away,
and she finally surrendered to the truth she'd been hiding
from since her first meeting with Luc. Marianne was
right. Falling in love did happen in the blink of an eye.

Because it was something new in her experience she hadn't realised what was happening to her. How could she have been so blind? It was plain, now, why she'd been miserable when Luc hadn't rung. Of course she was in love with him. Otherwise she wouldn't be here, like this, eager to spend every waking second of this weekend, and as many more weekends as possible in future, in his company. She was no teenager with a crush. Men had wanted to make love to her often enough. But to be desired in this subtle, cherishing way of Luc's was something she had never encountered before. And probably never would again.

'Then in that case...' she whispered, and felt his body tense, as though he were sure she would push him away. She knew that if she did he would let her go without argument. Wasting no more time on words, she touched Luc's lips with her own, in a caress which acted exactly as he'd predicted—like a match thrown on kindling. He received the kiss with disbelief, then kissed her wildly, hungrily, crushing her close, the building tension of the past two days exploding into a passion Portia had been given a mere foretaste of the night before.

Luc muttered incoherent words against her parted, gasping mouth, his hands stroking her feverishly through the silk of her shirt. Portia's schoolgirl French wasn't up to understanding most of it, but she no longer cared. She said yes to everything he was demanding as he took her by the hand and raced with her to the bedroom he'd omitted from his earlier tour of the flat.

Holding her fast in the crook of his arm, as though she might change her mind if he broke contact, Luc switched on a lamp and turned down the covers of his bed with his free hand, then turned her in his arms and looked down at her, his eyes oddly stern.

'You must know that I am in love with you, Portia,' he said in French, and a tremor ran through her as her brain translated.

'*Amoureux* is such a beautiful word,' she said breathlessly, knowing that he wanted her to reply in kind, but unable, yet, to put words to feelings she'd only just discovered for herself.

'It is you who are beautiful, Portia,' he said hoarsely, and threaded his fingers through her hair. 'I am on fire for you.'

Then take me, she said with her eyes, and Luc began to undress her with hands clumsy in their feverish hurry to dispense with the barrier of clothes which separated them. When she was lying naked in his arms at last, Luc gave a ragged sigh of pure delight and held her tightly with one hand, the other smoothing and stroking down her spine and her thighs until every part of her was in such close contact with Luc's taut body that Portia realised, for the first time, what it meant to be one flesh, even before their bodies were united. And, instead of the immediate, passionate union she craved, Luc was inexorable in his intention to withhold the final intimacy until he'd kissed and caressed every part of her into a state of longing so intense she was sure she'd lose her reason if he didn't take her soon. Even when he did, at last, he was tantalising as he made their union complete, his body taking possession of hers with a subtle, gradual progression designed to give both of them every nuance of pleasure it was possible for them to experience together. The sensations he induced were almost unbearably intense as the rhythm slowly grew faster, then progressively wilder, until the final cataclysm of pleasure overwhelmed her seconds before Luc finally relaxed the

iron grip of his own control and collapsed on her in utter
abandonment to the ecstasy of his own release.

Portia lay beneath Luc's weight like a butterfly pinned
to a board, so shaken and dazed she would have found
it hard to breathe normally even if Luc's body hadn't
been crushing the life out of her. He raised his head at
last, and with reluctance rolled over, taking her with him
so that she was held close in his arms, her head on his
shoulder. He pulled the covers over them, then lay with
one hand stroking her hair, giving Portia time to recover
some semblance of calm.

'That,' he said at last, sounding shaken, 'was the most
sublime experience of my entire life, *chérie*.'

Portia digested that in flattered silence, then twisted
up her face to look at him. 'How old are you, Luc?'

'Thirty-seven.' He smiled down at her. 'Am I allowed
to ask your age, Portia?'

'Of course. I'm thirty.'

He frowned. 'I thought you were younger than that.'

'I wasn't fishing for compliments,' she assured him.

'Nor do you need to.' The look in his eyes brought
heat rushing to her face. 'You must know that to me you
are the most ravishing creature I have ever met. That
first day in Turret House, you were so elegant in that
long coat and Russian hat I was captivated from the first.
Then at the hotel I surprised you in your robe, with that
wonderful hair cascading over your shoulders—' He
shrugged his broad shoulders. 'I was *bouleversé*. How
do you say that?'

'Bowled over?'

'Exactly.' Luc kissed her lingeringly. 'There was no
escape for you from the first, Portia. You belong in my
arms like this.' He paused, stroking a possessive finger
down her flushed cheek. 'Why did you ask my age?'

Portia's lashes dropped to hide her eyes. 'You must have had a fair amount of experience.'

'True. I am male, and normal. But I have never known such desperation to make love to a woman. Nor,' he added, his voice deepening, 'such rapture in achieving my desire.'

Portia's eyes turned up to his. 'You're very good at it,' she said bluntly.

He laughed delightedly. '*Merci beaucoup.* It would be strange if I were not experienced in love at my age.' He raised an eyebrow. 'Unlike you at your age, Portia.'

'Oh? Why do you say that?' she demanded, bristling.

'Because of this famous experience of mine.' Luc pulled her closer and kissed her again, refusing to let her break free. 'No. I will not let you go.'

'Then tell me what you mean,' she said crossly.

'Very well. You were a delight in my arms, Portia, so ravishingly responsive once you lost your natural caution. But other than your kiss of consent you instigated no caresses of your own.'

'Oh, I see,' said Portia ominously. 'You mean you're used to women who crawl all over you.'

To her indignation, Luc threw back his head and roared with laughter. 'No, no, Portia,' he said unsteadily at last. 'That is not what I meant.'

She glared at him. 'Stop laughing at me!'

Luc kissed the tip of nose and settled her more comfortably against him, one of his legs thrown over hers in an attitude of such overt possession Portia's anger was deflected. '*Chérie,*' he began, very seriously, 'when did you last make love with a man?'

Instead of blowing her top, and telling Luc Brissac to mind his own business, Portia sagged in his embrace like a deflated balloon. 'Why?' she said gruffly.

He cradled her close. 'The lady who introduced me to love was older than me. She taught me patience. But since then such patience has never been necessary, until tonight, with you. I wanted you so much it was difficult to take things slowly. I know it was not your first time, but it was plain that I must take care not to cause you pain.'

'When I was in college I had a boyfriend all the time I was there, but no one since,' she said tersely, and felt Luc tense with surprise against her.

He raised her face to his, his eyes narrowed. 'Did this boy injure you in some way?'

'No.'

'Portia, is that the truth?'

She nodded. 'We just went our separate ways after college, that's all. I haven't seen him for years. He went abroad to work.'

Luc stared at her in astonishment. 'No one else in all that time?'

'Is that so hard to believe?'

'Yes,' he said flatly. 'You are so beautiful, Portia. It is truly amazing that no man has tried to make love to you in all that time.'

She shrugged. 'Plenty tried. But up to now no one succeeded.'

'Then why was I granted such a gift, Portia?' he asked quietly.

She looked at him thoughtfully for a moment. 'Because you're the first man since then who's possessed even a flicker of sexual attraction for me,' she said with candour. It was only one reason among several. And the only one she was willing to admit to as yet. But from the look of exultation on Luc's face he was more than pleased with her admission.

'You do me great honour, Portia,' he said, very soberly, and slid out of bed to put on the towelling robe thrown across the back of a chair. He came round the bed and sat on the edge of it to take her hand, smiling indulgently.

'Do you wish to get up for dinner, Portia, or shall I spoil you and bring a tray for you in here?'

'Good heavens, no,' she said at once. 'Besides, I thought we agreed to cancel dinner tonight—' She stopped, flushing, as she realised that the thought of food was more attractive than she'd expected.

Luc chuckled, and bent to kiss her cheek. 'But making love makes one famished, *n'est ce pas*? Especially loving of the intensity we found together. We both expended much energy.'

'I'd rather not discuss it,' she said, colouring. 'Though I would like something to eat. But first I'd like a bath, please.'

Assuring her that she could have whatever she wished, Luc waved a hand at the bathroom door, announced that he would take a shower in the main bathroom, and left Portia to scoop up her scattered clothes and shut herself in a bathroom decorated in surprisingly minimalist style. Not that Portia had much attention to spare for it. She was too eager to sink into hot, pine-scented water.

When Portia emerged, Luc was waiting for her. He smiled and planted a kiss on each cheek, then on the tip of her nose.

'I was beginning to think you would never come out.' He eyed her challengingly. 'I did not think you would like it if I came in to assure myself nothing was wrong.'

'How do you know I didn't lock the door?' she countered.

His look almost made her back away. 'You need

never lock a door against me, Portia. I will never demand anything you have no desire to give.'

'If I didn't believe that,' she said very deliberately, 'I wouldn't have come here today.' She walked into arms which opened to receive her, and lifted her face to his. 'But I am here, and I'm very happy to give you a kiss, if you'd like one.'

After deciding on sandwiches as the quickest, easiest supper, the rest of the evening was spent sitting close together on the chesterfield in Luc's sitting room, with music as a background for their discovery of each other. They avoided the painful area of personal bereavement, but otherwise no topics were barred from their conversation as they explored the differences in their respective cultures, and discovered a surprising amount of common ground.

'What I can't understand,' said Portia much later, 'is why you're not married.'

Luc gave his usual expressive shrug. 'My mother desires this, and I came near to it once or twice. But never near enough to marry.' He ruffled her untidy hair. 'It is a mystery to me that you also are single.'

Her face closed. 'Marriage has never appealed to me.'

'Why not, Portia?'

'I like my life the way it is.'

'This life of yours must adapt now to include me,' he informed her.

She turned her face up to his. 'Is that what you want?'

He kissed her swiftly. 'Is it not obvious, *ma belle*, that I want it very much? It is not my usual practice to spend so much time in London. But in future you will keep your weekends free for me, *n'est ce pas*? And sometimes you could come to me in Paris.'

'Perhaps,' she said non-committally.

'I see I must use persuasion!' Luc scooped her up in his arms and strolled towards the bedroom. 'I know a very good place for that.'

She rubbed her cheek against his shoulder. 'You mean you're going to make love to me until I give in?'

'Yes,' he said matter-of-factly, but the altered rhythm of his breathing betrayed him, and when he came down beside her on the bed he threaded his hands through her hair and looked deep into her eyes. 'The truth is, *chérie*, that I need to make love to you again to convince myself I did not dream the first time.'

Portia was in full agreement, and made this clear in a way Luc found so ravishing that this time his self-control was less absolute. Portia was no longer passive, but grew progressively more adventurous with caresses of her own, causing such havoc that glory overwhelmed them again all too soon.

'Stay with me,' said Luc unevenly, when he could speak.

Portia was deeply tempted, but in the end she sighed and shook her head. 'I need to be at work early in the morning. In fact, I must leave soon. Will you drive me, Luc?'

He shook his head. 'I will ring for a taxi. Then I can hold you in my arms until we part.'

When they arrived in Chiswick Luc told the driver to wait and went up with Portia in the lift, taking her in his arms to kiss her all the way up to her floor. When they reached it he unlocked the door for her and kissed her again.

'I cannot bring myself to go,' he groaned, holding her cruelly tight. 'It will be a long, long week until I see you again.'

'Then stay,' said Portia recklessly.

He raised his head, his eyes glittering in astonishment. 'You mean that?' Without waiting for her confirmation he raced from the flat to pay off the taxi-driver, and minutes later they were undressing feverishly and making love again in Portia's bed. And this time they fell asleep in each other's arms, and only woke when Monday's dawn brought them back to reality.

CHAPTER NINE

WHEN Portia finally arrived at her desk that morning, much later than usual, Biddy took one look at her and made pointed comments about burning candles at both ends. 'I heard about this new eye-cream,' she added. 'Does wonders for circles under the eyes.'

Portia didn't care about marks under her eyes, or the fatigue that made her day's programme harder than usual to carry out. The February day was dark and bitterly cold, but in Portia's heart it was spring.

'Someone's happy in their work,' commented Ben Parrish, when he heard her humming cheerfully on her way out that night.

'It's spring,' she reminded him.

'It's something,' he agreed suspiciously. 'If I didn't know you better, Miss Grant, I'd say you were in love.'

'Me?' she said innocently. 'I'm married to my work, Ben. Goodnight.'

When Portia got home she ran to the telephone to find the message button winking on her machine, just as she'd hoped, and Luc's unmistakable accents telling her that it was late, that she should be home, and that he would ring again later. When he did Portia subsided into her armchair, her legs dangling over the arm, as Luc demanded details of her day, her health, and told her how much he wanted to be there with her, holding her close and—

'Don't,' implored Portia breathlessly.

'Are you missing me?' he demanded.

'Yes.'

'Good. Keep that thought in your mind, *chérie*. And tell this Joe Marcus you are not available any more.'

'He's just a friend, Luc!'

'He's a man. If you need a friend keep your time for the so charming Marianne,' he ordered.

'How about you?' she retorted. 'How do I know you're not seeing women every night in Paris?'

He laughed indulgently. 'If I were, would you be jealous?'

'No. I'd just make sure I wasn't here next weekend.'

'I want no other woman, Portia,' he said, suddenly serious. 'I thought I made that very clear yesterday.' He let out a deep, audible breath. 'Yesterday was so beautiful for me. To hold you in my arms all night was a privilege beyond my wildest dreams.' He paused, listening. 'Are you still there, *chérie*?'

'Yes,' she said huskily. 'I'm here.'

'And you will be there when I arrive on Friday night,' he stated.

'Yes.'

Luc groaned. 'It will be the longest week of my life.'

Portia's week was a succession of cripplingly busy days, followed by evenings highlighted by Luc's call. Some nights, due to pressure of work, his call came later than usual, and Portia watched the clock with tense, anxious eyes, unable to eat, or read, or even watch television until she talked to him. Sometimes, when she found it hard to get to sleep in the bed she'd so recently shared with Luc, she made resolutions about keeping her head. Then forgot them the moment she heard his voice again.

When Joe Marcus rang her in work one day, to see if

she fancied a film that night, Portia braced herself and told him she'd met someone.

'So? It's not the first time.'

'Actually it is. Like this.'

'Are you telling me some guy's finally breached the famous Grant defences?' he demanded.

'It's not the way I'd have phrased it myself, but, yes, I do mean that.'

'Look, Portia, you know I'm fond of you. So take care, eh? Make sure he's on the level.'

'Of course he is,' she said crossly.

'Then bless you, my child, have fun.' He paused. 'But if you need me any time, you know where I am.'

Marianne's reaction was far more satisfactory. She demanded that Portia spent Thursday evening with her, to keep her up to date on the French connection.

'Ring me on my cellphone number tomorrow, Luc—if you are ringing me,' said Portia that evening. 'I'm going out.'

'Who with?' said Luc instantly.

'Marianne. Though Joe did ask me.'

'And what did you say?'

'That I'm seeing someone.'

'That is a very lukewarm way of describing our relationship,' said Luc hotly. 'Tell him I am your lover, Portia.'

'I can't tell him that!'

'Why not? It is the truth.'

'It's not a word I feel comfortable with. But don't worry, Joe understands perfectly.'

'Good. Otherwise I would make it clear to him myself.'

Because Marianne was the only person in the world

she could confide in about Luc, Portia thoroughly enjoyed their evening together.

'I've got a half-bottle of champagne to drink with supper,' said Marianne with satisfaction, and fixed Portia
with a searching blue eye. 'So. You've finally found
someone you like.'

Portia smiled luminously. 'It's a lot more than that.
I'm head over heels in love.'

Marianne's eyes widened. 'Head over heels!'

'You told me I was wasting time.'

'Yes. But if I hadn't met the tasty Monsieur Brissac
in person I'd find it pretty hard to believe you'd taken
my nagging to heart so quickly.' Marianne bent to plant
a kiss on Portia's cheek. 'I'm glad. I was beginning to
think you'd never take the plunge.'

'Well, I have, with a vengeance.' At the mere memory
of it colour rose in Portia's cheeks, but for once
Marianne tactfully made no comment, and even took
herself out of the room when Portia's phone rang with
the expected call from Luc.

'Now I know it's true,' said Marianne, returning to
resume her dinner. 'I recognise the starry-eyed look. I
see it in my own mirror since I met Hal.'

Portia changed the subject to ask for news about Dr
Courtney, and gazed at her friend, wide-eyed, when
Marianne confessed that the champagne had a dual pur-
pose.

'We're getting married,' said Marianne, and held out
her left hand. 'Those starry eyes of yours never even
noticed my brand-new ring.'

Portia should have been on standby at the weekend, but
Ben Parrish, keeping his promise to make up for her
consecutive visits to Turret House, took over for her.

'Because,' he said, wagging a finger, 'something tells me you've got plans this weekend. Dare I suggest they involve a man?'

'You may, and they do,' said Portia, hurling her belongings into her bag. Then gave him the surprise of his life by reaching up to kiss his cheek before plunging out into the freezing fog to make for the car park.

It was a slow drive home, and Portia was worried by the time she finally reached the flat. But there was no message from Luc to say his flight had been cancelled. To pass the time she prepared their meal as far as possible without actually cooking it, then embarked on the lengthy process of making herself as beautiful as possible for him. But by the time she was ready Luc was overdue. She told herself that the plane was delayed, or he couldn't get a taxi. Then why didn't he ring? Portia fiddled with the table in the kitchen, putting the cutlery straight and rearranging tulips in a small pottery jar. She gave a stir to the creamy sauce she would pour over the cooked chicken breasts when he arrived. She pushed buttery breadcrumbs around in a frying pan, then took them off the heat and checked her watch for the hundredth time.

At last she went back into the sitting room and turned on the television, then hit the Ceefax button to search for news of flights into Heathrow from Paris. Her heart sank when she saw there was up to two hours' delay on some, and others had been cancelled. Next time, she decided fiercely, he could come by train through the Channel Tunnel. No fog problems there.

By the time Luc was two hours overdue Portia had dusted and polished every inch of the flat to keep herself occupied, and convinced herself he'd either crashed into the Channel, or changed his mind about coming.

Memories of the previous weekend came flooding back, and she began to curse herself for breaking the rule she'd kept so long where men were concerned. She was on the point of throwing the half-prepared meal away when the buzzer rang and Luc's husky, weary voice asked her to let him in.

Her heart thumped wildly as she waited for the small bell which announced the arrival of the lift. She opened her door and Luc, in formal overcoat and suit, threw down his overnight bag and took her in his arms without a word of greeting, kissing her with a hunger she responded to with the same need, relief and joy flooding her in equal force as he held her close.

'Mon Dieu,' he said hoarsely at last, raising his head. 'I thought I would never make it.'

'Why didn't you *ring*?' she demanded breathlessly.

'Your line was engaged. Who were you talking to?' he demanded, gripping her shoulders fiercely.

'No one—' she gasped, then surrendered again to his kiss, euphoric in her joy that he was here. Tired, pale, and in need of a shave. But here.

'While I waited in line for a taxi at Heathrow I rang you again, but all I could get was the engaged signal,' he went on, still holding her close.

'I was so *worried*,' she said, burying her face in his shoulder. 'In the end I thought you weren't coming at all,' she added indistinctly.

Luc turned her face up to his. 'You thought I would not come?'

Portia nodded, her colour rising at the look in his eyes, and Luc pulled her close and kissed her until neither of them could breathe.

'This, and this, was all I could think of all week,' he

said roughly. 'Are you mad? Nothing would have kept me away.'

She smiled radiantly and danced away from him into the kitchen. 'I must put the dinner in.'

Luc took off his coat, and loosened his tie as he followed her. He leaned in the doorway, watching as she poured the sauce over sliced chicken and fresh green broccoli. 'I did not wish you to tire yourself cooking a meal after a long working day, *mignonne*.'

Portia scattered the crisp buttered crumbs over the dish, then slid it into the oven. 'There.' She smiled at him. 'Would you like a drink?'

'Not if it is the wine your friend brought!'

'How you do go on about Joe,' she said severely. 'I spent a long time in consultation about the wine I chose. It's white, dry, French and very expensive, so I hope it will do.'

'If I drink it with you, Portia, it will taste like nectar whatever it is,' he assured her, and accepted the glass she filled for him. 'To us.'

'To us,' she echoed.

Luc drank some of the wine, then frowned suddenly and went over to the phone 'I have solved the mystery, Portia. The receiver is not in place.'

She stared at the phone, then at Luc, her eyes full of remorse. 'What a fool I am! I could have saved myself a very bad couple of hours if I'd thought to check.'

He frowned. 'I also tried your cellphone, Portia, but with no success. By this time I was insane with worry, certain something was wrong.'

Portia ran to her bedroom for the large handbag she used for work, and rummaged through it, then rejoined Luc, her colour high. 'I must have left it in the office. I was in such a hurry to get home tonight.'

'Why, *chérie*?' he said caressingly. He put down his glass and held out his arms. 'Were you as eager to see me as I am to see you, by any chance? Come. Kiss me to make up for all the anguish you caused me.'

Later, when they'd eaten the dinner Luc pronounced delicious, and drunk the wine she'd paid such a scandalous price for, he rose from the table and held out his hand to her.

'I am tired,' said Luc, his eyes locked with hers.

'Then perhaps you should go to bed,' she said unevenly.

'You must be tired also?'

'Yes. A little.' Which was a lie. Portia had never felt less tired in her life.

'First, I would like to shower,' he informed her.

'Right. You do that while I clear up.'

Portia made herself take her time over washing dishes and putting them away. She was certain Luc would want to take her to bed the moment he emerged from the bathroom, but no way could she bring herself to undress in readiness. Which, she discovered, was just as well, because when Luc rejoined her his hair was damp from the shower, and he'd shaved, but though his long, narrow feet were bare, he was wearing black needlecord trousers and a fresh shirt. She smiled at him, secretly deeply grateful. Much as she wanted him to make love to her the feeling was still new enough to need tenderness and care.

'Now,' he said, holding out his hand. 'Come and sit with me on your sofa and tell me about your week.'

Portia curled up against him as he drew her close. 'Part of me was just marking time, waiting for this. The other part was out selling houses as usual.'

Luc ran a caressing hand through her hair, winding

gleaming strands of it round his fingers. 'It was the same for me, Portia.' He laughed a little. 'I am like a school-boy with a crush. I could not sleep. After the magical night together in your bed my own was cold and lonely.' He paused. 'Though do not jump to conclusions, *chérie*. It is not just our bed I want to share, but your life. One day—because I know I must proceed very carefully with you—I want us to be together all the time.'

Portia lay very still. All the time? She raised her head to look at him. 'I think we should get to know each other better before we think of anything—'

'Permanent?'

'If that's what you mean, yes.'

'What else would I mean? A love affair for a while, then *adieu*, and on to pastures new?' He frowned at her, his eyes suddenly cold. 'Or is that your preference, Portia?'

She detached herself and moved away, to curl up in the other corner of the sofa. 'My preference,' she repeated quietly, 'is to take things one step at a time.'

Luc thrust a hand through his damp hair, his eyes narrowed. 'You mean you dislike the idea of a permanent relationship?'

'I didn't say that. I just consider it sensible to know each other better before—'

'Sensible!' he said with scorn. 'What man in love wants to be sensible? I am crazily in love with you, Portia—but it is very obvious that you do not return my feelings.'

She looked down at her tightly clasped hands. 'Actually, I do,' she said inaudibly.

Luc moved along the sofa and caught her by the shoulders. 'Say that again,' he demanded.

Portia took in a deep, unsteady breath, and looked him

in the eye. 'If I didn't have feelings for you, Luc Brissac, last weekend would have been very different.'

'You mean you would not have made love with me?'

She nodded.

'So your emotions must be involved before you give yourself to a man?'

'Presumably.'

He scowled and shook her slightly. 'Presumably? What kind of word is that?'

'The kind,' she said tartly, 'that you use when the situation has never occurred before.'

Luc's hands relaxed a little. 'What are you saying, Portia? Perhaps my grasp of the English language is not as good as I imagine. Explain.'

She sighed impatiently. 'I'm trying to. I was actually thinking of marrying the boyfriend I had in college, but it didn't work out. And then my mother died, and my life changed a lot, and since Tim I've never had the slightest inclination for anything more than the odd kiss or two.' She gave him a wry little smile. 'Then I met you, and fell in love for the very first time.'

Luc pulled her onto his lap and kissed her fiercely. 'Why could you not say that before? A man needs to know that his feelings are reciprocated.'

'It comes easier for you,' she muttered.

'Is that what you think?'

'You told me you were in and out of love all the time when you were young,' she reminded him.

'But I am not so young now. And it is a long, long time since I have been in love. And never before like this. Do you believe that, Portia?' he added very quietly.

'I want to believe you,' she said honestly.

He stood up and set her on her feet. 'If you are not sure it is obvious I must find a way to convince you. I

want you so much, Portia. I longed for you every minute
we were apart.'

'It was the same for me too,' she assured him, and
reached up to kiss him. 'Last time that was enough to
start the fire,' she whispered.

'This time also,' he said hoarsely, and took her by the
hand. 'I will not carry you to bed, because I wish to save
my energies for better things.'

'Better things?' she queried, dancing away from him.

'The very best in life!'

CHAPTER TEN

ALL too soon the demands of their professional lives interrupted the weekend idylls. A fortnight later Luc rang to say he was urgently required in Provence to cinch the deal on the property the owner was now willing to sell at a more realistic price.

'This week my diary is full, so I must go at the weekend. Fly to Paris on Friday and drive down to Provence with me, *chérie*.'

'Oh, Luc, I'd just love to, but I can't this weekend,' said Portia, anguished. 'It's my stint on standby. Ben's taken over for me twice lately. I can't ask him again.'

'You mean it is two weeks before we can be together again?' he said, incensed. 'This is impossible, Portia. I cannot exist like this.'

She went cold. 'You mean you want to end it?'

'No, I do not!' There was a sudden silence. 'Is that what you want?' he said very carefully.

'*No!*'

'*Bien*, because I meant,' he said with passion, 'that I want more of you, not less, you maddening woman.'

Portia let out the breath she'd been holding. 'I want it too,' she said sedately.

'If,' said Luc, with dangerous calm, 'we were together at this moment, *ma belle*, I would make you admit so much more than that.'

'I'm sick with disappointment, if you want the truth.'

'Ah, *chérie*,' he said caressingly. 'You cannot know how good I feel to hear you admit this. I am disappointed also. If I could I would delegate the Provence deal to someone else. But the owner of the château is being difficult. She insists on my personal attention—'

'I understand, Luc,' she said quickly. 'Really I do. But I'll miss you. Badly.'

'Then it is time we did something about it.' He paused. 'Can you take a day or two off the following week, Portia?'

'I suppose I could,' she said, thinking it over. 'I've got some time owing to me.'

'Then fly to Paris, and I shall drive you to St Malo.' He paused. 'I wish you to see Beau Rivage.'

'Luc's taking you home to Mother?' said Marianne in awe. 'Doesn't hang about, does he? You haven't known him long.'

'About a month or so less than you've known Hal,' Portia reminded her.

Marianne grinned. 'True. But almost from the first Hal and I have been seeing each other at least five days a week. A bit different from these mad, passionate weekends of yours.'

Portia coloured. 'How do you know they're passionate?'

Her friend shook her smooth blonde head pityingly. 'It's blindingly obvious, love. To me, anyway. You've never been like this before. Ever.'

'He wants me to live with him, Marianne.'

'And are you going to?'

'I don't know.' Portia shrugged. 'Maybe my trip to France will make my mind up. His mother may hate the sight of me.'

'Will that put you off?'

'I'd rather she didn't. But maybe she's old-fashioned. She might think of co-habiting as living in sin.'

Marianne frowned. 'But if Luc's taking you home to Mother, surely he's got marriage in mind?'

Languages had never been Portia's favourite subjects in school. But as a little surprise for Luc she embarked on a crash course to improve her French, with conversation tapes she played in the car wherever she went. A couple of long, stop-over trips to Cornwall and the north of England did wonders for her French conversation. Because Luc's English invariably deserted him the moment he took her to bed, she was determined to understand every word he said when he made love to her.

To Luc's surprise she told him she'd rather not fly to Paris. And that because she much preferred to travel on the Channel by ferry, rather than under it in the train, she would take her car to St Malo and drive herself to Beau Rivage.

'Only make sure you're there before me,' she implored. 'I'm nervous about meeting your mother.'

Luc laughed indulgently and told her that of course he would be there before her. 'Waiting impatiently until you are in my arms again, *chérie*.'

On the drive to Portsmouth that evening, after putting in a hard day's work to leave her desk as clear as possible, Portia began to regret her chosen form of travel. After a restless, disturbed night, nothing to do with weather conditions, Portia drove off the ferry at St Malo next day to find Luc waiting for her, dressed in jeans and a heavy sweater, his hair ruffled in the brisk breeze. His eyes lit up as he spotted her, and he jumped in the car when she halted, causing a hold-up in the traffic leaving the ferry as he kissed her hard before letting her drive on.

'I didn't expect you to be here at this hour,' she said breathlessly, her heart thudding at the devouring look he turned on her. 'You faxed me the directions to Beau Rivage—'

'But I could not wait, so I asked one of the gardeners to drive me in.' He laid a hand on her thigh, his fingers caressing it through the fine wool of the suit she'd bought specially for the occasion. 'You look so *soignée*, so perfect. Too perfect—I want to tear the pins from your hair and bring it tumbling down on your shoulders. Why did you wear it up today?'

'To look as presentable as possible to meet your mother, of course. Will she approve of me?'

Luc's face shadowed. 'I must warn you that my mother is not at her best with strangers. Do not worry if she seems formal. You have *my* approval, which is all that matters.' His fingers burned on her thigh. 'Ah, *chérie*, it is an age since I touched you—'

'Luc, please,' she said huskily. 'How do you expect me to drive when you say things like that? Give me directions!'

Portia's first sight of Beau Rivage was a glimpse of tall chimneys over the high walls surrounding the property.

'Which is not large,' said Luc, as they drove through the main gates. 'No more than eight hectares or so.'

It seemed large enough to Portia. She drove carefully along a formal carriageway, through gardens which sloped down to the river, with a statue here and there as focal points. The house itself was large and imposing, with walls picked out in granite and tall windows positioned to overlook the traffic on the river.

'You are very silent,' remarked Luc, as he helped her out of the car.

Portia gave him an expressive look. 'It's not surprising. You home is dauntingly grand, Monsieur Brissac. I'm speechless.'

'You don't like it?'

'Of course I do. It's very, very beautiful.' She smiled wryly. 'But I feel I should pay to see round it.'

Luc nodded matter-of-factly. 'People do. During the summer it is open to the public. The money is welcome. Maintenance is constant on a house built almost three hundred years ago.'

He picked up her bags and led the way through the double glass-paned doors into a flagged hall, with a central pillar and a stone staircase with a banister of wrought-iron as delicate as lace. As he dumped the bags down a woman in an expensively simple blue wool dress emerged through a door at the back of the hall.

Her greying blonde hair framed a fair, cold face which bore no resemblance at all to the olive-skinned features of her son. She came towards her guest with a faint, regal smile, her eyes taking in the quality of Portia's trousers and jacket briefly before resting on her face.

'Welcome to Beau Rivage, Miss Grant. I am Regine Brissac. You must be tired after so demanding a journey. Was the crossing very rough?'

Portia took the hand held out to her, relieved there was no need for her newly acquired fluency in the language of her hosts. Madame Brissac spoke English as well as her son. 'How do you do? The crossing was rather choppy but I'm a good sailor.'

'This is why you chose to travel by ferry?'

'Yes—I dislike flying,' said Portia, aware that Luc

was watching his mother intently. 'Won't you call me by my first name, *madame*?'

'If you wish.' Regine Brissac turned to her son. 'Bring your guest to the kitchen for coffee.'

'We shall take these to Portia's room first,' said Luc, with slight emphasis on the name. He picked up the bags. 'Then we shall join you in the kitchen.'

'Of course, *mon cher*.' Madame Brissac smiled glacially at her guest. 'It is a pity your stay will be so short—Portia. Luc tells me your job is very demanding.'

'She is a partner in a very grand estate agency,' said Luc, looking his mother in the eye. 'With the various pressures of our careers it takes much organisation to spend time together.'

'Then you must make sure she enjoys her stay here at Beau Rivage.'

Chilled by his mother's cool welcome, Portia shivered a little as she followed Luc up the curving staircase and along a corridor which led towards the back of the house.

'I thought you would prefer one of the rooms kept private from the public,' said Luc rapidly. He opened a door, and dropped her bags on the floor of a room with tall windows looking out over the river. Portia was allowed only a quick glimpse of beautiful faded carpet and a boat-shaped bed before Luc swept her into his arms.

'I trust you were not desperate for coffee, because I am desperate for this,' he muttered against her mouth, then kissed her with a heat she delighted in after the icy reserve in his mother's manner. Luc raised his head a fraction to look into her eyes. 'Tell me, Portia,' he said unevenly, 'did you long for me as I longed for you?'

'Yes,' she said simply, and gave herself up to an embrace which got out of hand, so quickly Luc put her away from him with unsteady hands, his breath ragged.

'I want nothing more than to go to bed with you right now, but—'

'This is your mother's house, and we can't do that,' she finished for him.

'It is *my* house,' he corrected her with hauteur, then shrugged wryly. 'But you are right. It will not do to linger here too long. My mother would not approve if I make love to you at this hour.'

Or at any hour, thought Portia, as they went back downstairs. It was too soon to decide that Madame Brissac actively disliked her, but it was obvious that the lady had reservations about the foreign guest her son had invited to stay.

Luc took Portia's hand to lead her into the kitchen, which was a vast room with one end fitted with modern appliances and a scrubbed table. At the other end a fire crackled in a large hearth, with a group of comfortable chairs drawn up to it and a long table close by, surrounded by dining chairs.

'Perhaps you would care to sit close to the fire,' said Madame Brissac politely. 'Our Breton springs can be very chilly, *n'est ce pas*?' She waved a hand towards a woman preparing vegetables at the far end. 'Clothilde, this is Mademoiselle Grant from England.'

Clothilde was small and round and in her forties, with a pleasant smile and a rosy face. *'Bonjour.'*

'How do you do?' said Portia, deciding not to air her French quite yet.

Luc seated her chose to the fire and brought her a cup of the coffee his mother poured, then collected his own cup and hooked a chair nearer to Portia's with his foot, giving his mother a warning look she chose to ignore.

'Clothilde baked the brioche this morning, *mademoiselle*,' she said. 'Would you care to try it?'

'I'd love to,' said Portia warmly, and cast a smile at the industrious servant. 'It looks delicious.'

'Did you eat breakfast?' demanded Luc.

'There wasn't much time. I just had coffee.'

'But why did you not say?' said his mother at once. 'Clothilde shall make you an omelette—'

'No, please,' protested Portia quickly. 'The brioche is perfect.'

'As you wish,' said Madame Brissac. 'I trust your room is to your liking?'

'It's lovely,' said Portia, avoiding Luc's eye. 'Such a wonderful view.'

'*Bien.* Later Luc shall give you a tour of the house.'

'I'd like that very much.'

They chatted politely together, but after half an hour Luc got up and held out his hand to Portia.

'Come. I shall take you on the grand tour. Only you, of course, being a privileged guest, shall see far more than the clients who pay.'

Portia thanked Madame Brissac formally for the coffee, complimented Clothilde on the brioche, then escaped with Luc.

He began the tour of his home in the formal grand salon. Portia looked round her in silence, trying not to feel daunted by the museum-like effect of crystal chandeliers and tapestry chairs, fragile gilded tables and boule cabinets filled with pieces of rare porcelain.

'Your mother doesn't like me at all,' she told Luc.

He shut the door and took her hands. 'It is just her way. Do not trouble yourself. The important thing for you to remember, *ma belle*, is that *I* adore you. So much

I think these few days will not be as relaxing as my
mother believes.'

'Why?' said Portia, knowing why, but needing him to
tell her.

'Because I shall be forced to employ much cunning
to have you all to myself. And even now I must not kiss
you as I want to, because then your lips will be swollen
and your cheeks red, and your eyes will grow heavy with
the wanton look I cannot resist.'

Portia breathed in sharply, and detached her hands.
'No more talk like that, please, Monsieur Brissac. For
now let's just enjoy being together while you tell me
about the room. I'm determined to make intelligent, informed comments on everything I see to impress your
mother at lunch.'

Luc laughed indulgently, and took his time over dis-
playing his home, pointing out certain pictures of interest, telling her which were his mother's favourites. 'The
most valuable were sold, of course, but I have since
bought others she likes very much. She is also very
proud of the panelling in here,' he added, as they entered
a formal dining room. 'It was made by Breton carpenters
on leave from their usual occupation of shipbuilding.'

The panelling formed the perfect background for a
table set formally with sparkling crystal, Limoges china
and silver flatware on an embroidered cloth, with a porcelain bowl of fresh spring flowers as the finishing touch.

'Do you eat all your meals here?' asked Portia, thinking of the meals she'd given him at her tiny kitchen
table.

Luc laughed, and kissed the tip of her nose. 'No. We
eat most meals *en famille* in the kitchen. My mother
insists that we dine in here tonight in honour of your
company, but lunch will be eaten at our kitchen table.'

He looked down at her steadily. 'But I will not enjoy that as much as the meals I eat at yours, Portia.'

She smiled luminously, touched that he'd sensed her qualms. 'How very graceful, Monsieur Brissac.'

He shrugged. 'No, just truthful, *chérie*. Now let us proceed.'

By the time the tour of Beau Rivage was over Portia just had time to unpack and tidy herself before Luc fetched her for lunch.

'This time,' he said, when she opened the door, 'I shall avoid temptation and remain outside.'

'Very wise,' approved Portia, and closed the door behind her.

'It is hard to be wise when I am mad with longing to hold you in my arms!' His eyes lingered on her face as they made for the stone staircase. 'You look very beautiful, but also very pale. I think you worked many hours extra this week.'

She nodded. 'To make up for the days I'm taking off. I felt a bit guilty about taking a holiday just as business is really hotting up.'

'But now you will enjoy it,' he commanded.

'I will,' she assured him, and he paused, taking her hand before opening the kitchen door.

'Why will you enjoy it?' he asked softly.

'Because I'm with you,' Portia whispered, giving him the answer she knew he wanted.

Luc's eyes flamed in response as he brushed her cheek with a caressing fingertip, then he opened the door and Portia, feeling like Daniel braving the lions' den, prepared to face her first meal at Madame Brissac's table.

In their absence the fire had been replenished and the table laid for three, the silver and china only a little less than in the panelled dining room.

'Ah, *bon*,' said Madame Brissac, appearing from an adjoining larder. 'I was about to send Clothilde to find you. Tell me your opinion of Beau Rivage—Portia.'

Glad she could say, with complete truth, that it was a quite wonderful house, Portia assured her hostess she was grateful for the privilege of seeing over it. 'Is help readily available?' she asked. 'It all looks so immaculate.'

'Some local women come in during the visitors' season, but at this time of year I manage with Clothilde and her two married daughters.' Regine Brissac turned to her son. 'Since we will drink cider with our lunch, Luc, I think an aperitif would not be wise beforehand. Unless,' she said, turning to Portia, 'you would care for one, of course?'

Portia was deeply tempted to say yes, just to be awkward. 'No, thank you, *madame*,' she said politely, and smiled at Clothilde as the little woman put down a vast bowl of green salad and a platter of bread.

'It is a very light lunch,' announced Madame Brissac, indicating the slices of terrine on their plates. 'We Bretons are known for our cider, of course, so I thought you would enjoy our chicken in cider jelly. We serve it with pickled onions and *cornichons*, or gherkins, as you say in English.'

Portia respectfully surveyed the perfectly aligned pattern of chicken and vegetable slices in their jellied casing. 'This looks too exquisite to eat,' she said, as Luc helped her to salad.

'But you must, *chérie*,' he said firmly. 'You are losing weight.'

Aware of hostile reaction to the endearment by her hostess, Portia was glad of the covering flurry of activity as she accepted oil and vinegar and bread before beginning on the terrine, which possessed a strong flavour all of its own, due to the dry, fermented cider which gave it its particular personality.

Both Luc and his mother drank cider with the meal, but Portia kept to mineral water, afraid cider might be the last straw for a digestion coping with a combination of tension, pickles and the thinly veiled hostility of her hostess.

Conversation grew slightly easier when Portia showed sincere admiration for those areas of the house Luc had said meant most to his mother. Portia paid compliments to the panelling in the dining rooms, and the tapestry chairs in the grand salon, deeply thankful for Luc's guidance when Madame Brissac confessed that the most recent covers had been created with her own needlework.

'You do not sew, *mademoiselle*?'

'I can mend things, but I've never tried my hand at tapestry or embroidery.'

'In the winter the evenings are long,' said Madame Brissac pointedly. 'My tapestry gives me occupation, since I see so little of my son.'

Luc shot an angry look at his mother. 'I come to see you as often as I can, as do Ghislaine and Amélie and their families.'

'Of course,' agreed his mother, unruffled. 'Let me give you more terrine, *mademoiselle*. It takes three days of preparation to achieve the perfect flavour.'

Which gave Portia no choice but to accept a second slice she found hard to finish, particularly when Madame Brissac confided that calves' feet poached in the stock with the vegetables ensured that the jelly set properly. And afterwards, when the very special cabinet pudding of brioche with crystallised fruits and jam was served,

Portia was unable to refuse that, either, when she was informed it was Clothilde's speciality.

'Though I made the custard—the *sauce Anglaise*—for our guest's benefit,' observed Madame Brissac.

By the time lunch was over, and coffee served by the replenished fire, Portia could hardly keep her eyes open.

'You must rest for a while,' said Madame Brissac with a hint of command.

Portia was only too happy to agree, though it was the lunch, rather than her journey, which had done the damage. A contrast to her usual hurried sandwich, she thought ruefully, as she went alone up to her room. Luc's help had been requested by his mother, over some business matters to do with reopening the house for the summer, and with his parent's watchful eye on them he merely smiled down at Portia as he saw her to the door.

'One hour only,' he warned. 'Then we shall go for a walk in the garden.'

'After which we shall have some English tea,' promised Madame Brissac graciously.

'Thank you, I'll enjoy that,' said Portia, finding it an effort even to smile.

She fell asleep almost at once, and slept soundly for almost an hour before she woke to look at her watch and leapt out of bed to dress and tidy herself before Luc came to find her.

She was halfway down the stairs when he came in from the garden, looking windblown, with more colour in his face than usual. His eyes lit with the familiar possessive glow as he watched Portia run down to join him.

'You are on time,' he said softly as he kissed her. 'Were you afraid I would come to your room if you were late?'

'Yes,' she said bluntly. 'You know your mother wouldn't approve.'

'She makes this very clear,' he said grimly, and took her hand. 'She invented a task to keep me with her when you went upstairs.'

Portia nodded. 'I thought so. Is she always like this when you invite people to stay?'

'No.' He opened one of the glass doors to let her out into the garden. 'Because my guests are always men, or married couples. You are the only woman I have asked here to meet her.'

Portia stared at him in deep dismay as they went along a walk lined with lime trees. 'I wish you'd told me that before.'

Luc frowned, bringing her to a halt. 'Before what?'

'Before I came. Otherwise—'

'Otherwise you would not have come,' he said impatiently, and resumed walking. 'I knew that. But I wanted so much for you to see Beau Rivage.' His eyes took on a possessive gleam as he waved a hand at their surroundings. 'When my father bought it, I was already sixteen years old, but the moment he drove me through the gates I was enslaved.'

'I can understand that,' she said with feeling.

They paused at the low wall bordering the lawns, where the occasional, skilfully placed statue stood out against a backdrop of trees and shrubs framing views of the River Rance. The breeze was stronger here, and colder, and Portia shivered slightly.

'You are cold,' said Luc, taking her arm. 'Come. We shall go round to the other side of the house to admire the kitchen gardens, then you shall drink your tea. I brought it specially from Paris. Just for you, *ma belle*.' Luc eyed the curls the breeze had plucked from her tightly coiled hair. 'Tonight, Portia, indulge me. Leave your hair down.'

'She shook her head. 'I'd rather not, Luc. I'll feel uncomfortable with my hair all over the place.'

'Do it for me,' said Luc, in a tone which quickened her pulse.

'Oh, all right,' she muttered unwillingly.

'You will do as I ask?'

'It was more an order than a request,' she said tartly, then smiled at him. 'But for you, anything.'

Luc's eyes lit with a molten look which took Portia's breath away. '*Mon Dieu*, I want so much to make love to you! I will come to your room tonight.'

'No,' she said quickly. 'Please. Not here in your mother's house—'

'It is *my* house,' he said harshly. 'And I want you.'

Portia made no attempt to hide the longing in her eyes. 'And I want you. But not here. Don't ask me to, Luc. Please.'

He seized her hands. 'Are you saying I must wait until next time we meet before I can make love to you again?'

'Yes,' she said flatly. 'I am. I shouldn't have come. I don't belong here—'   '*Ne dis pas des bêtises!*' he said explosively. 'I mean—'

'I know what you mean. And it's not nonsense, Luc. In London I feel we meet as equals. Here I'm very conscious of our different backgrounds.'

'Do you mean because your parents were honest artisans?' he said, and flung away to stare blindly at the view of the river through a short colonnade of pines. 'Do you think I care about that?'

'No,' said Portia disconsolately. 'But your mother does.'

Luc turned and took her face between his hands. 'My mother does not rule my life for me, Portia. Nor is she "to the manner born", as you say. She comes from respectable Breton farming stock. And my father was an architect who left Paris to practice in St Malo to please her. Beau Rivage was in such disrepair he bought it for less than the price gained for our house in Paris. So no more talk of not belonging, Portia. You belong to me.' His lips met hers in a hard, emphasising kiss, then he took her hand. 'Now. Before we go in we must admire *les chartreuses*. They are my mother's pride and joy.'

CHAPTER ELEVEN

THE *chartreuses* were a series of small gardens enclosed by stone walls angled to catch the sun for the vegetables and espaliered fruit grown there. Portia, feeling a great deal happier after Luc's lecture, was charmed with them, and told his mother so over tea served in the grand salon.

'They were in ruins when we came here,' said her hostess, looking gratified.

Discussion of Madame Brissac's labours in her vegetable gardens not only came as a surprise to Portia, but eased the strain of partaking of the finest Darjeeling from fragile porcelain in a formal, chilly room, where everything smacked of restrained grandeur, from the Aubusson carpet to the mouldings on the ceilings.

'But do you do the digging as well?' asked Portia.

'I make sure she does not,' said Luc. 'I pay local men to do the rough work in the gardens.'

'I concern myself with planting and nurturing—and instructions,' said his mother, and went on to describe the types of vegetable she had experimented with over the years to add to the staple crops of potatoes and artichokes common to the region. 'Edouard, Luc's father, was no gardener. In the spare time from his profession he was concerned only with restoring the building.' Her cold blue eyes met Portia's very deliberately. 'Since his death Beau Rivage is my life.'

Later, in her room, Portia took no pleasure in getting ready for dinner. No matter how strongly Luc felt about her, Regine Brissac's message had been very clear. If

Portia Grant had any fancy ideas about coming to live at Beau Rivage with Luc she could forget them as far as his mother was concerned.

After the revealing little session in the grand salon Portia had needed time to herself before dinner.

'Why?' Luc had demanded at the foot of the stairs. 'It is two hours or more until dinnertime. Why waste it alone, without me?'

Portia had looked at him levelly. 'I always need some time to myself, Luc, wherever I am. Normally our time together on weekends is so brief I don't expect—or need—this. But I don't leave until Tuesday morning, so I need space to myself for a while. I'm going to take a long bath, read a bit, and spend a lot of time making myself presentable for tonight.'

Luc had looked down his nose, his black brows drawn together. 'Very well, Portia. I will allow you your space. But I shall expect you downstairs at seven-thirty, and not a moment later.'

It was a few minutes short of that when Portia finally decided she was as ready as she was ever going to be for dinner with Madame Brissac. Her dress was severe in cut, made from velvet of a rich bronze shade which echoed the hair she swept back in wings above her ears and secured at the crown of her head with a gilt clasp, leaving the rest to curl on her shoulders as a compromise to Luc's wishes.

As she reached the head of the stairs Luc paused on his way up to gaze at her. He was dressed in one of his superbly cut suits, a dark blue silk tie at the collar of his gleaming white shirt, and her heart missed a beat at the sight of him, her eyes questioning as they met the oddly sombre look in his.

'You are so beautiful,' he said softly.

She smiled radiantly and went down to join him. 'So are you.'

Madame Brissac, wearing diamond studs in her ears and a plain black dress, was waiting for them in a small room kept private from the public.

'Come in, Portia,' she said politely, her eyes taking in every last detail of her guest's appearance. 'We use my own little room tonight, to enjoy a fire. I trust you had a good rest?'

'Yes, thank you, though I didn't actually sleep. I read for a while before my bath.' Portia spied a frame with a half-finished tapestry stretched on it. 'May I look, *madame*?'

'Of course. Luc, give Portia an aperitif.'

Luc handed a glass of wine to Portia, who took it with absent thanks as she looked at his mother's impressive handiwork. 'You're very accomplished, *madame*,' she said with sincerity.

Regine Brissac shrugged. 'Only in matters domestic. I have never been obliged to earn my own living as you do.'

Something pejorative in her tone stiffened Portia's spine, and, sensing it, as usual, Luc took her hand and drew her down beside him on the chaise longue drawn up to one side of the hearth, retaining her hand in his when she tried to pull free. Madame Brissac, sitting straight-backed in a small velvet chair, directed a cold glance at their clasped hands and announced that dinner would not be long.

'So what do we eat tonight?' asked Luc.

He never addressed his mother as Maman, Portia noticed.

'In honour of your guest I chose a truly regional dish.'

Madame Brissac smiled blandly at Portia. 'You like fish?'

'Very much,' said Portia, with fond memories of tuna flan. Dinner promised to be less daunting than lunch. With no calves' feet involved.

Luc began asking questions about his nephews and nieces, and described them to Portia, and with a topic so dear to his mother's heart the time passed pleasantly enough until Madame Brissac left them to supervise in the kitchen.

When they were alone Luc put his arm round Portia and drew her close. 'This is obviously difficult for you, *chérie*. We should have spent the time at my Paris apartment, where we could be alone together.' He sighed. 'As must be very plain to you, my mother and I are not close.'

Portia looked up at his sombre face. 'Why not?'

'Various reasons.' He touched a hand to her cheek. 'I will not burden you with them.'

When they were seated in the panelled dining room, with Luc at the head of the table, Clothilde came in with a vast steaming platter she set down with care in front of Madame Brissac.

'*Merci beaucoup*, Clothilde,' said Luc warmly, as the smiling little woman left the room.

'Luc says your appetite is modest, Portia,' said his mother as she served the meal. 'So there are no *hors d'ouevres* tonight. This is a dish of salt cod, soaked for several days in advance, then fried and served with sautéed potatoes, red peppers and artichokes.'

Luc handed Portia her plate. 'You like artichokes?'

'I've never tried them,' she confessed, and when they were all served took care to eat very slowly, just in case she was pressed to more. The flavours of the meal were more to her taste than expected, but so strong she was grateful when Luc supplied her with mineral water to augment her dry white wine.

While they ate Madame Brissac, very much the *grand dame* entertaining her guests, informed Portia that in times past the Bishop of Rennes would bless the fleet which sailed from St Malo to the New World in search of cod. The fleets would be gone for months at a time, some of them never to return.

'But the original owners of this house,' said Luc dryly, 'made their fortunes in less respectable manner.'

'Really?' Portia smiled at him. 'How?'

'They were corsairs—the polite term for licensed pirates—who sailed from St Malo to engage both in normal trade and to attack enemy ships and sell their plunder.'

Madame Brissac gave him an admonishing look, then told Portia that in time the St Malo corsairs became more respectable, and were given exclusive trading rights with the French East India Company. 'They moved out of the fortified town itself to build *malouinieres*, beautiful country houses like Beau Rivage, outside the city walls.'

'How romantic,' said Portia, fascinated.

'To look back on now, maybe,' said Luc, smiling at her. 'But I doubt that the corsairs themselves were romantic in any way at all.'

This time when Madame Brissac offered a second helping Portia refused with polite regret, adding that the meal had been delicious, but very filling. When Luc also declined, his mother rang the bell, and Clothilde appeared to set a chocolate-coated confection garnished with whipped cream beside her employer.

'This chestnut loaf is very light, Portia, and much

loved in Brittany,' said Madame Brissac as Clothilde bore the dinner plates away.

'This is utterly delicious,' said Portia after tasting her portion, and learned, unsurprised, that the dish had been made in advance and garnished just before serving.

No fast food at Beau Rivage, thought Portia, resigned. Everything she'd eaten so far had needed days of preparation, according to Madame Brissac, who was making it very plain that Luc's guest had caused a lot of extra work for the Beau Rivage household.

After dinner they returned to sit by the fire in the intimate little room Portia much preferred to the formality of the grand salon.

'You do not speak French, Portia?' said Madame Brissac as she poured coffee.

Portia smiled noncommittally. 'I studied it in school, of course, but nothing to compare with your command of English, *madame*. Or Luc's.'

Regine Brissac smiled complacently. 'When the children were young I engaged an English nanny. A most superior woman, with teaching skills. She came here with us from Paris, and stayed until she retired. We had all studied English in school, of course, but Miss Brown taught us the art of conversation.' Her face shadowed. 'It was useful when the house was a hotel for a while. But Luc uses it most these days.'

It soon became apparent that Madam Brissac had no intention of leaving her son alone with his guest. At eleven Portia rose to her feet, thanked her hostess for the meal, and wished her goodnight. But this time Luc rose to accompany her, something in his face deterring the objection his mother obviously burned to make.

In silence Luc escorted Portia upstairs and along the corridor to her room, and when they reached it he closed

the door behind them and took her in his arms, holding
her close in an oddly passionless embrace.

'Forgive me,' he whispered into her hair. 'It was a
mistake to bring you to Beau Rivage yet.'

Portia leaned back a little to look up into his face.
'Yet?'

'Until you and I are together officially, when our relationship is *fait accompli*.'

'Personally, I doubt your mother will ever approve of
me.'

Luc's eyes narrowed. 'She will, in time. I shall make
very sure of it. But as yet this is new to her. I have
brought no others to meet her.'

'Others?'

He shrugged. 'I am not a boy, Portia. Of course there
were other women in my life from time to time. But you
are the only one I have ever wanted in this way.' He
drew in a deep breath. 'It was not my plan to mention
it so soon, but you must realise I want you for my wife,
Portia.'

When she gazed up at him in shocked silence his eyes
glittered in disbelief. 'You do not want me?' he demanded arrogantly.

'You know I want you!' she said passionately. 'But I
won't marry you.'

Luc released her and stepped back, looking as though
she'd struck him. 'Tell me why, Portia,' he commanded.

She hugged her arms across her chest. 'It's nothing
personal.'

'Nothing personal!' he repeated, his face suddenly taut
with anger. 'To me a rejection of such a nature is very
personal. Are you telling me you are married already?'

'No.' Portia turned away in despair. 'I've been a fool.

I should never have let it get this far. I never dreamed you'd actually want to *marry* me.'

'I am so frivolous a character?' he asked bitterly.

'No. But I thought you'd just want a love affair! With no strings, and no recriminations when it cooled down.' She turned to face him. 'As it will, Luc. What we've found together is wonderful, but it couldn't last at such intensity.'

'The "intensity", as you describe it,' he said with passion, 'is because I never see enough of you. If we were married, or even living together, this fire I feel for you would not die as long as I breathe, but it would diminish in time. It is hard for me to believe at this moment, it is true, but it will not matter because our minds are as much in rapport as our bodies.'

Portia gazed at him with imploring pain-filled eyes. 'Luc, please leave me alone now. When—if—you come to see me again in London I'll give you the explanations you want. But not here.'

He looked at her in silence for a moment, then gestured at the bed. 'If I made love to you now—'

'It would make no difference,' she assured him.

Luc's face hardened. 'Then I shall not trouble you further,' he said coldly, and strode from the room, closing the door behind him with a finality which put an end to Portia's self-control.

She stripped off the new dress, tears pouring down her cheeks as she hung it away. She pulled on a nightgown and sat huddled on the edge of the bed, wishing she'd never laid eyes on Luc Brissac. She mopped her eyes, sniffing miserably. For the first time in her life she was hopelessly in love, and that, of course, was the point. It *was* hopeless. She'd been a fool to let things go so far, and an even bigger fool to come here to Beau Rivage.

Giving up any attempt to sleep at last, Portia rose very early next morning and packed her clothes. When she was dressed in the new trousers and jacket she coiled up her hair very tightly, then made up her face in a vain attempt to obliterate the effects of the night.

Ideally Portia would have liked to steal away from Beau Rivage without a word to anyone. Knowing this was out of the question, she went downstairs early, intent on a private word with Luc before she said goodbye to Madame Brissac. After that, no matter what Luc said, she would leave to wait for the ferry in St Malo.

Halfway down the stairs she overheard conversation coming from the small sitting room. For a moment Portia hesitated, reluctant to eavesdrop, but when she heard her name she put her luggage down very quietly, surprised to find she could understand most of what was obviously a telephone conversation.

'Luc has been very successful,' said Madame Brissac with gloating triumph. 'He has achieved exactly the result I desired. The girl is obviously besotted with him. Unfortunately,' she added angrily, 'she has bewitched him in turn. He is madly in love with her. A great mistake.'

There was a long pause, then Madame Brissac interrupted angrily, 'No, Ghislaine, I am not wrong. And of course it was her fault. As far as I am concerned she killed him.'

There was another pause, then Madame Brissac continued, 'Luc is on his way to you at this very moment. I told him you'd had an accident, so he will be furious. Nevertheless, keep him there with you as long as you can.'

Regine Brissac rang off, then came hurrying out of the room to find Portia standing like a statue, halfway down the stairs. 'Ah. Mademoiselle Grant,' she said, without turning a hair. 'You are early.'

'Yes,' agreed Portia dully. 'I'm afraid I overheard your conversation.' She looked down very directly into the cold blue eyes. 'You know, then.'

'Of course I know,' said Madame Brissac scornfully. 'Otherwise Luc could not have carried out my plan. It was I who...' She paused, searching for the word. 'Who instigated the search.'

Portia stared at her blankly. 'Search?'

'I paid an investigator to look for you,' said the other woman matter-of-factly.

'But why?' Portia stared at her in astonishment. 'What possible interest did I have for either of you? I'm afraid I don't see the connection.'

Madame Brissac's face took on a sceptical expression. 'Then perhaps it is time we were honest with each other, *n'est-ce-pas*? You were leaving?' she added, catching sight of the luggage. 'Without telling Luc?'

'If necessary. I got up early to drive to St Malo to catch the ferry. I was going to leave a note if no one was around.'

'You shall not leave yet,' said Madame Brissac imperiously. 'Luc has gone on an errand to his sister. Before he comes back you shall listen to me. It is time your association with my son was revealed in its true light.'

Portia walked slowly down the stairs. *'Madame,'* she said formally, as she confronted her hostess in the hall, 'there's no need for this. I'm not going to marry him.'

Regine Brissac stared at her blankly. 'What is this?'

'Luc asked me to marry him, but I refused.'

'He asked a woman like you to be his wife?'

Portia felt like an actor strayed into the wrong play. The entire conversation seemed unreal as Regine Brissac turned on her like an avenging fury. 'A woman like you has no right to a man like my son.'

'*Madame,*' said Portia, icily formal to hide her anger, 'since my presence is obviously causing you distress, I'll leave now. I'm grateful for your hospitality, but—'

'No,' interrupted Madame Brissac. 'First you and I will have a little talk.'

'I can quite see, *madame,*' began Portia, 'why you consider me an unsuitable wife for Luc.'

'I imagine you can,' sneered the other woman.

'When I told Luc about my early life at Turret House—' Portia broke off. 'You know of the house, *madame*?'

'Oh, yes,' was the bitter response. 'It was your home, I believe?'

'Not my home, exactly. I merely lived there for a time when my mother took the post of housekeeper to the owner.' Portia braced herself. 'When I told Luc about it I had to leave a month out.'

'What happened during this month?' demanded Regine Brissac.

Portia gazed at her in despair. 'I haven't the faintest idea.'

'What do you mean?'

'I remember returning to Turret House after my mother's funeral, then nothing until a month later, when an ambulance arrived to take the owner to hospital.' Portia met the other woman's eyes without flinching. 'Mr Radford died in hospital later that day. I left Turret House the same evening and went to stay with my friend's family.'

'You are telling me you have no recollection of that September at all?' asked Regine Brissac in disbelief.

Portia looked at her, startled. 'You know it was September, *madame*?'

'Who should know better than I?' said the other woman bitterly. 'So. What caused this convenient gap in your memory?'

'The doctor I consulted believes I can't remember because I'm afraid I caused Mr Radford's stroke and subsequent death.' Portia shivered. 'This, plus a whole month of my life I can't account for, is why I won't marry Luc.' She frowned, puzzled. 'But why did you have me investigated, *madame*? Did you know Mr Radford?'

'No,' said the other woman with supreme indifference. 'I care nothing for this man, nor the manner of his dying. Me, I do not believe this fairy tale about your lost memory. But,' she added with significance, 'if it really is missing, it is possible I can help you.'

Portia stared into the implacable eyes. 'What do you mean?'

'I mean,' said Regine Brissac, breathing rapidly, 'that right here, in Beau Rivage, I have something that may restore your memory.'

Portia's chin lifted. 'Then perhaps you'd be kind enough to show it to me.'

'Very well. Follow me up to the *grenier*.'

The familiar, formless dread began to rise inside Portia like a smothering mist as Madame Brissac led the way up to the Beau Rivage attic, where she unlocked a door and held it open, motioning Portia inside.

With deep reluctance Portia went into the room, then stopped, transfixed, at the sight of two huge photographs on the wall opposite the bed. She stared incredulously, her heart thudding at the sight of herself in a brief bikini, smiling and sunburnt, her hair blowing in the wind. The other photograph showed a handsome boy with long blond hair, posed against a sailing dinghy drawn up on a sandy beach. The likeness to Regine Brissac was unmistakable.

Portia stared wildly from one young face to the other. Then the inexorable mist rose up and finally swallowed her.

CHAPTER TWELVE

WHEN Portia regained consciousness Madame Brissac was kneeling beside her.

'*Bon*, you have come round. Can you get up?'

With Madame Brissac's help Portia got to her feet, then stood swaying, her eyes on the photographs. She swallowed convulsively, and turned away, accepting the woman's helping hand as they went slowly back down the stairs.

'I will help you to your room, *mademoiselle*,' said Madame Brissac, sounding subdued.

Portia nodded dumbly, glad to rest on the pretty bed, even more thankful when she was left alone. But after a moment or two Madame Brissac returned with a glass.

'Drink this cognac,' she said briskly. 'You are white like a ghost.'

Portia sipped obediently, coughing as the spirit hit her throat. 'Thank you,' she said, and subsided against the pillows.

Madame Brissac looked less militant as she pulled up a chair close to the bed. 'I regret making you faint, *mademoiselle*, but now you must own to knowing Olivier.'

Portia nodded. 'The boy in the photograph looks very much like you, *madame*, so I assume he's your son. He called himself Olly. I never knew his other name. He worked at Ravenswood that year with the other French students.'

'Luc insisted, as part of his training. Olivier was there

161

until the end of this September you say you cannot remember.'

Portia's mind felt like a jigsaw puzzle, with a maelstrom of discarded pieces flying together all at once, forming a picture she couldn't bear to look at. 'Where is Ol—Olivier now?'

'My beloved son is dead,' said Regine Brissac fiercely. 'And you killed him.'

Portia jerked upright, staring at the woman incredulously.

'He was driving home from a party and lost control. He had been drinking,' added Madame Brissac defensively, 'because you broke his heart.'

'*Madame,*' said Portia, very deliberately. 'I hardly knew your son.' She thrust a hand through her hair, her head spinning with the onslaught of returning memories. 'I used to go down to the cove for an hour some afternoons, when it was fine. And Olly often sailed round in his dinghy. But always with one of the other waiters crewing for him. He was charming, and good company.' She met the other woman's eyes without flinching. 'But it was nothing more than that.'

'It was nothing to you, perhaps, but Olivier was so much in love with you that when you disappeared so suddenly he was inconsolable,' said Regine Brissac bitterly. 'My child would spend hours up in that room, staring at your photograph.'

Portia was coming to terms with so many things at once she felt sick. The brandy tasted acid at the back of her throat as pieces of the jigsaw jostled to fall in place. 'Poor boy,' she said unsteadily. 'I'm very sorry he died, but it was nothing to do with me. He was years younger than me. I honestly never thought of him in that way.'

'Then why did you not tell him that?' cried Madame

Brissac. 'He came home ranting of this girl, that you had been lovers and he wanted to marry you. He pleaded with me to try and find you.'

'Madame,' said Portia very gently, 'to me your son was a charming schoolboy. We were *not* lovers. We never exchanged so much as a kiss.'

Regine Brissac gave her a scornful glare. 'I do not believe that. For years I burned with the desire to find you, to tell you what you did to my son—'

'But I did nothing, *madame,'* said Portia gently. 'I'm deeply sorry Olivier died, but I had no idea he felt anything for me. He was just a boy.'

Madame Brissac's eyes glittered as she stared at the girl on the bed. 'Life is strange, *n'est ce pas*? Fate led Luc straight to you when he bought his London flat from the agency where you work.'

Portia's eyes narrowed suddenly. 'You mean Luc knew who I was before we met?'

'But of course,' Madame Brissac said gloatingly. 'When he decided to buy Turret House I instructed Luc to combine the business with the pleasure and make you fall in love with him.'

'Then you must be very happy,' said Portia, feeling sick. 'He did exactly as you wanted. Tell me,' she added bitterly, 'what was the precise plan, Madame Brissac? After I was caught in the trap you set me, what was to happen then?'

For the first time the other woman looked less sure of herself. She eyed Portia defiantly. 'I told Luc to—to seduce you, then abandon you. To inflict the pain Olivier suffered. Then my revenge would have been complete.'

Portia nodded slowly. 'I see. That's why Luc persuaded me to talk about myself, of course. To learn about Olivier. But I couldn't oblige.' She shrugged. 'Not that it matters. Even if I had remembered Olivier I doubt I'd have talked about him. I hardly knew him.'

Madame Brissac gave a choked sob, and put her head in her hands.

Portia eyed the downbent head with detached compassion. 'I wish I had remembered Olivier, *madame*. It would have saved a great deal of trouble, one way and another.' She sighed wearily. 'I hope you won't think me rude, but I'd deeply appreciate a little time alone now.'

'Yes, of course.' Madame Brissac got to her feet, looking haggard. She turned at the door. 'When Luc returns I will send him up to you. If I was mistaken about you,' she added with obvious effort, 'I apologise.'

When Portia was alone at last she got up and went to the bathroom to splash cold water on her face. Afterwards she made a few repairs, then looked at her watch blankly. So much had happened since she'd first got up, yet it was still only a little after nine. She controlled a sudden urge to throw herself on the bed and cry her eyes out, and went down to the hall instead, relieved to find her bags waiting there. After looking in Madame Brissac's small sitting room Portia went to the kitchen, then took a peep into a few other rooms, but with no result. She hesitated, then returned to the hall, wrote a brief note, and placed it on one of the hall tables.

In minutes she'd stowed her bags away in the car and was on her way into St Malo, praying tidal conditions would allow the ferry to leave on schedule. Her prayer granted, Portia was halfway across the English Channel before she finally relaxed. Right up to the last moment she'd been afraid Luc would appear to block her escape. But for the moment she couldn't cope with thoughts of Luc. Or of his mother. She needed time to come to terms with memories which had begun to rush back the moment she'd seen her photograph alongside Olivier Brissac's in the *grenier* at Beau Rivage.

During the crossing Portia went over and over the events of that lost, terrible September. She had chosen to spend the summer with her mother, instead of going to Italy with Marianne and her brother. Then, when Christine Grant had died suddenly of a heart attack, Portia had been desperately grateful to the instinct which had told her to stay home. The day of the funeral, still numb with grief, Portia had agreed listlessly when Lewis Radford had asked her to take care of Turret House for a week or two until he found a new housekeeper. And until today, in the attic at Beau Rivage, the period from her mother's funeral to the day she left Turret House for good had remained a complete blank.

In some ways, thought Portia, as the ferry sailed homeward, she wished it still was. Now, she thought with a shudder, she could recall only too clearly how Lewis Radford's manner had changed. While her mother had been alive he'd hardly deigned to acknowledge Portia's existence. But after the funeral he'd seemed to be watching her all the time, his eyes on her every move. Reminding herself constantly of the debt she owed him, Portia had told herself she was imagining things. But she'd felt Lewis Radford's eyes on her just the same, crawling like spiders on her skin, and though the weather was hot she'd taken to wearing long-sleeved shirts buttoned to the neck, and pushed a heavy chest against her door at night. And prayed that the morning would bring a reply to one of her job applications, or news of Marianne's return.

Portia had lived for the hour or two she took off each afternoon to swim and sunbathe in the cove. Sometimes

Olly, the charming young French waiter from the hotel, would sail round in his dinghy with one of the other young waiters, and Portia had enjoyed the brief, pleasant interludes in youthful male company which contrasted so pleasantly with Lewis Radford's.

She had always returned early from the beach every afternoon, long before Lewis Radford was due home from his legal practice, but that last day Portia had found him waiting in the hall, brandishing binoculars, his face suffused with anger. He'd spat terrible names at her, accused her of consorting with men on the beach, and told her it was now his turn. He'd seized her arms in a bruising grip and pushed her into the lift, ranting and raving like a maniac, terrifying Portia when he sent the lift up to the turret room he'd always kept locked. He'd flung her inside it, and Portia had stared in horror at the pornographic studies of young girls plastered all over the walls of the empty room. And in pride in place huge shots of herself and young Olly and his friends on the beach.

One look was all Lewis Radford had allowed her before he'd pounced on her, tearing at her clothes, bellowing it was time she paid her debt in full at last. She'd fought him off like a wildcat and run for the stairs, careering madly down the spirals with Lewis Radford in hot pursuit. Portia had burst out into the hall, screaming as he grasped her shoulder. The grip had slackened, he'd given an ugly choking sound, and collapsed, unconscious, on the worn red carpet.

Portia shuddered as she remembered feeling for his pulse to make sure he was alive. She had rung for an ambulance immediately, and afterwards, half out of her mind with horror and shock, had gone back up in the lift and torn down all the pictures, taken the remaining film from the camera standing on a tripod at the window. When she'd been satisfied nothing was left she'd taken the bundle down to the kitchen. She'd added her shirt, stuffed everything into the Aga bit by bit, and sent all evidence of Lewis Radford's hobby up in smoke.

During the voyage, as she looked back on that terrible afternoon, Portia still had no idea how long the ambulance had taken to arrive. When the paramedics asked what had happened she'd been unable to tell them a thing. Four weeks of her life had remained stubbornly blotted from her mind until she'd seen her photograph with Olivier Brissac's at Beau Rivage, and found the key to unlock the door she'd slammed shut in her memory.

When Portia finally arrived home in Chiswick after the drive from Portsmouth, she felt drained, desperately tired, and in no mood to answer the phone she could hear ringing as she unlocked the door. She let the machine take over and, just as expected, Luc's urgent voice demanded that she pick up the phone. She listened for a moment, then gave in and picked up the receiver.

'Hello, Luc,' she said wearily. 'I've just got in.'

'*Mon Dieu*, Portia, why did you run away?' he demanded, incensed. 'Can you imagine my feelings when I returned to find you gone?'

Portia could. Easily. 'I left you a note. Didn't you find it?'

'Of course I found it! Was it supposed to make me feel better?'

'Oddly enough,' she informed him bitterly, 'at that moment your feelings were not my main concern.'

There was a pause.

'Of course. Forgive me,' said Luc tightly. 'I am so angry with my mother I am not thinking clearly. I had forbidden her to mention Olivier and her obsession during your visit, you understand. Yet she deliberately lied about an accident to my sister to get me out of the way. Just so that she could take you up to the *grenier*. I apologise for her, and the distress she caused you—'

'No need. I'm grateful to her.'

'Grateful?'

'Yes. Thanks to your mother I'm now clear about a lot of things. Very interesting things,' Portia added significantly.

Luc breathed in audibly. 'You mean you are angry with me because you discovered that I deliberately set out to—to—'

'Seduce me?' she suggested coldly.

'If you mean I found great joy in your arms, then you are right, Portia. You expect me to feel sorry for that?'

'No,' she retorted, stung by the arrogance in his tone. 'I don't *expect* anything from you, Luc.'

'You know very well that I love you—'

'No,' she said inexorably. 'You want me. There's a difference.'

'Have you forgotten I talked of marriage?' he demanded hotly. 'Yet even before you knew about Olivier you refused me. Why, Portia? Is marriage to me so unthinkable?'

'You won't understand this,' she assured him, 'but when you first mentioned it there were certain reasons why I couldn't accept your proposal. Those, oddly enough, no longer apply, because my memory's decided to come back. Now I've got a different set of reasons for turning you down.'

'Tell me what they are!'

'For one thing you set out to seduce me out of revenge—'

'I did *not* set out to seduce you, Portia. Can you not accept that? Revenge was my mother's goal, not mine.' He took in a deep breath. 'Listen to me, please. I was growing more and more concerned for my mother's mental health. So when, by chance, I discovered you worked at the Whitefriars Agency, I decided to get to know you. But not out of revenge. I was convinced that if I heard your side of the story it would rid my mother of her obsession about Olivier's death.' He sighed heavily. 'It was never my intention to fall in love with you—'

'Nor I with you,' she retorted, stung. 'Goodbye, Luc.'

'Good*bye*?' he said incredulously. 'I cannot believe this. Are you saying you never wish to see me again?'

Portia pushed a tired hand through her hair. 'I had a lot of time to think on the crossing and the drive home. It became clearer with every mile that the gap between us is a lot wider than just the English Channel. Until I arrived at Beau Rivage I hoped it didn't matter. Now I know it does. You're a smooth operator, Luc. I really believed you were in love with me—'

'It is the truth,' he interrupted harshly. 'I keep telling you. Revenge was my mother's desire, not mine. I could never hurt you in such a way.'

'But you have, just the same. And I'm not only hurt, but furious with myself for being so gullible. I played right into your hands, didn't I? You made a fool of me. I can't turn off a switch and stop loving you right away. But at this moment, Luc Brissac, I dislike you intensely.' She cut the connection, took the phone off the hook, then switched off her cellphone, firmly putting herself beyond the reach of electronic communication.

* * *

Portia immersed herself in work when she got back to
Whitefriars, parrying enquiries about her early return
with the excuse of a cancelled holiday. It was no surprise
to find there was a message on her machine from Luc
when she got home that night. He sounded tired, the
husky, accented voice affecting her so strongly she almost relented and rang him back. But instead she rang
Marianne, and asked to see her as soon as possible.

'Right now, if you like,' said Marianne promptly.
'Hal's on call tonight. Why aren't you in France?'

Later Marianne listened in dumbfounded silence while
Portia gave her a detailed account of the entire visit,
ending with the photographs in the Beau Rivage *grenier*,
which had triggered recall of her lost September. But
long afterwards, when Marianne had stopped cursing
Lewis Radford and had finally run out of questions, she
eyed Portia searchingly and asked once more.

'But apart from all that, are you sure you never want
to see Luc again?'

'No.'

'You mean no, you don't, or no, you're not sure?'

Portia let out a long, unsteady sigh. 'Part of me wants
to see him more than anything else in the world. But the
other part hates the way he deliberately set out to make
me love him.'

'And succeeded. Because you do.'

Portia couldn't deny it. 'Illogical, I know, but I'd find
it easier if he *had* been thirsting for revenge. The fact
that he was humouring his mother makes it all so much
worse, somehow—harder to forgive.'

'I don't suppose she told him to take you to bed!'

'As long as *madame* achieved her ends I don't think
she was too fussy about the means.'

'Glory be! Just as well she's not going to be your

mother-in-law, then,' Marianne smiled thankfully. 'I get on rather well with Hal's mother.'

'You get on well with everyone,' said Portia with affection. 'So when's the wedding?'

'This very summer, and you're chief bridesmaid.'

Portia was very grateful for Marianne's wedding. The preparations helped fill the terrible aching emptiness left by Luc. At first he was merciless in his efforts to contact her, leaving messages on her phone and at the office, even sending faxes asking her to return his calls. Afraid to risk the seductive effect of Luc's voice, Portia arranged for a new unlisted telephone number, instead of leaving her phone off the hook every night, and bought a new cellphone. And she contacted Joe Marcus again, and arranged to have dinner with him. Only to learn that the occasion was an opportunity for Joe to tell her he was getting married.

'Joe Marcus, the serial bachelor?' said Portia, laughing, then insisted on treating him to champagne to celebrate.

She was genuinely glad for Joe, who was a good friend and would make his lucky lady a great husband. She would miss her outings with him. But for the moment going out with any other man who wasn't Luc was pointless, anyway. From now on she'd stick to evenings spent with friends of her own sex.

Inevitably Portia's security system broke down. She answered her telephone during Biddy's lunch hour one day and found she was listening to Luc's unmistakable accents.

'At last, Portia,' he said in triumph. 'Listen to me—'

But Portia, heart hammering, put down the phone,

then rang through to Reception and gave instructions regarding her non-availability to a Monsieur Luc Brissac. Just as she'd feared, one word from Luc was enough to breach all the defences she was trying so hard to build against him.

For days after that Portia expected Biddy to tell her Monsieur Brissac had asked for her again. But eventually she realised that this wasn't going to happen.

'He's given up,' she told Marianne despondently.

'I don't blame him. Do you mind?'

'Of course I don't.'

'Oh, come on, Portia, this is me you're talking to.' Marianne looked her in the eye. 'Ring him. Tell him you've thawed.'

'Not a chance.'

'You prefer your life the way it is?'

Portia smiled ruefully, unable to lie to Marianne. 'No. I prefer it the way it was, before I went to Beau Rivage.'

In her heart of hearts, something barely admitted to herself, let alone to Marianne, Portia had fully expected Luc to fly to London when his phone calls failed to reach her. When he didn't her life felt horribly empty without him. She filled it with visits to the cinema and theatre, and one weekend went to the party Joe Marcus threw to celebrate his engagement to his Sarah. But when she got home the flat seemed more lonely than before. At which point Portia looked the unwelcome truth in the face. She missed Luc so badly she no longer resented the reason for their first meeting. Because no man, not even Jean-Christophe Lucien Brissac, could have made her fall in love against her will.

The moment Portia arrived in the office next morning, she put through a call to Luc's Paris office, and in careful French gave her name and asked if Monsieur Brissac would speak with her. After a wait Portia was informed that Monsieur Brissac was away for a few days, and would *mademoiselle* care to leave a message? *Mademoiselle* was so disappointed she could hardly muster enough French to decline.

Portia had prepared herself for the fact that Luc might refuse to talk to her. After her recent behaviour she could hardly complain if he did. But the discovery that he was away came as such an anti-climax Portia sat staring blindly at the work on her desk, until Biddy came in to remind her she was due at the first viewing of the day.

Portia was brooding over an uneaten sandwich in her office during the lunch hour when Ben Parrish came in, yawning, and perched on her desk.

'I don't suppose, Miss Grant, ma'am, that you could possibly do me a favour?'

Portia eyed him warily. 'It depends, Mr Parrish, sir, on the nature of the favour.'

He gave her a wheedling smile. 'The thing is, Portia, it's my anniversary, and my five-thirty client can't get here until an hour or so later. Sue booked dinner in our favourite eating place weeks ago. She'll blow her top if I'm late getting home.'

'As long as you don't expect me to go chasing off to some remote part of the British Isles.'

'Now would I do that?' he said injured.

'Ben, if the alternative was losing a sale, of course you would.' Portia relented and grinned at him. 'So where do you want me to go?'

'Darkest Kensington, to sell "a beautifully presented maisonette with south-facing terrace and patio garden" et cetera, et cetera. The owners are on holiday, so it's all yours. Are you sure this won't interfere with your plans?'

'Very sure,' she sighed. 'My dance card's empty to-night.'

After a final session with Biddy Portia had half an hour to fill before driving to Kensington, and spent it on her face and hair to make a good impression on the people interested in the expensive property.

Portia let herself into the smart maisonette with the key Ben had given her, and went on a quick tour of inspection before her clients arrived, making notes of the features most likely to recommend the property to a prospective buyer. She was eyeing a rather gaudy specimen of modern art over the drawing room fireplace when the buzzer rang. She pressed a button to hear a voice with a pronounced East End accent announcing the arrival of a Mr and Mrs John. Portia pressed the release button and opened the door. Then stood staring at the tall, elegant figure of the man she'd been trying to contact that very morning.

'Luc?' she said incredulously, and looked out into the street. 'What are you doing here? I'm expecting clients—'

'I am your client,' he informed her.

'So who spoke on the intercom?' she demanded, fighting to hide her ecstatic pleasure at the sight of him.

'The taxi driver.' He smiled crookedly. 'If I had announced myself you would not have let me in.'

Not ready yet to tell him how mistaken he was on that point, Portia led the way into the drawing room. 'Have you given up your place in Hampstead?' she asked politely.

'No.'

She frowned. 'You need two places in London now?'

'No,' he said absently, his eyes moving over her with such unconcealed hunger Portia flushed, finding it hard to believe that Luc Brissac was actually here in the irresistible flesh.

'Then what's your interest in this place?'

Luc tore his gaze from her with obvious effort, and looked around him indifferently. 'I have no interest in it at all.'

Portia blinked. 'Am I missing something? If you don't want a flat why are you here?'

Luc turned his green, hungry gaze on her again. 'It was the only way I could think of to see you. Are you not proud of your power over me? That I should go to such lengths to see you again?'

'How did you arrange it?' she asked, not really caring how, only why.

'Your Mr Parrish was most helpful.' Luc moved nearer. 'He told me you changed your telephone numbers.'

'Did he now?' said Portia militantly.

Luc's eyes glittered. 'You have been very cruel, Portia. Did you enjoy your revenge?'

She stared at him, shocked. 'I wasn't out for revenge. I was just angry.' Her eyes fell. 'And hurt.'

'I know. I wanted so much to make amends. But you would not talk to me. And I was sure that if I came to your apartment you would tell me to go away.'

Portia, not nearly so sure, raised her eyes to his. 'Probably.'

His mouth twisted. 'So I employed a different strategy, and lured you here tonight. Are you angry?'

'No.' Portia smiled a little. 'Not angry.'

'Are you saying you are glad to see me?'

'I rang you this morning,' she said elliptically.

Luc's eyes blazed incredulously. 'You rang Paris? Why, Portia?'

'Last night I made a discovery.' She looked at him steadily. 'I've taken all this time to discover something that was staring me in the face.'

'And what is that?'

'That no man, not even you, Luc, can *force* a woman to fall in love with him.'

He nodded gravely. 'That is true. Love is very dangerous. There is no defence against it. I went to meet you at Turret House out of concern for my mother. But from the moment I first saw you I was determined to put an end to my mother's dramatic nonsense about revenge. Can you believe that, Portia?'

'I want to,' she admitted.

'I just wanted you for myself.' Luc moved nearer still. 'I still do. So very much, *chérie*.'

Portia's heart skipped a beat. 'Shall we discuss it somewhere else?' she said breathlessly. 'It doesn't seem polite to stay in someone else's house under the circumstances.'

Luc looked at her for a long moment. 'Do you know a restaurant nearby where we can dine?'

'Is that what you want?'

'Not exactly, Portia.' He smiled crookedly. 'But at this moment it is *your* wishes that concern me most.'

'I've got my car,' she said, collecting her briefcase. 'I suggest we buy some food on the way back to my flat. There are things I need to say to you I can't discuss in a restaurant.'

On the drive to Chiswick, Portia talked determinedly about Marianne's wedding, the upsurge in the property market, and asked Luc about the work in progress on the château he'd recently acquired. But Luc was abstracted with his replies, apparently content just to look

at her, undermining her concentration with the gaze he
kept fixed on her face throughout the journey.

Portia called in at a delicatessen on the way, and
bought French bread, ham and pastrami. When they got
to the flat she gave Luc a bottle of wine to open, and,
determinedly brisk, told him to sit down while she tossed
a salad, sliced bread and arranged the meat on a plate.

'Not much like your Breton cuisine, I'm afraid,' she
said lightly.

Luc held her chair for her, then poured the wine. 'As
you remember, Portia, *charcuterie* like this is very much
to my taste' He looked her in the eye as he seated himself opposite her. 'Not that it matters what I eat, now I
am with you again. But I must not assume too much, I
know, just because you agreed to talk to me.'

She smiled a little. 'Not your usual way, Luc.'

'No,' he agreed sombrely. 'Normally I am not so pa-
tient. But I learned a lesson at Beau Rivage, Portia.
When I returned to find you gone I—' His jaw tightened.
'I do not possess the English to describe my feelings.'

'You understand why I couldn't stay?'

'Of course I do. When my mother confessed that she
had disobeyed me I was insane with worry until I knew
you were safe.' His eyes held hers. 'And then you would
not talk to me.'

Portia reached out a hand to touch his. 'Let's eat, then
afterwards we'll talk, Luc. The things I want to say are
not exactly an aid to digestion.'

Luc tensed, his eyes narrowed in suspicion. 'I will
obviously not like these things. Do they concern our
relationship, Portia?'

'No. Not directly, anyway.'

He relaxed slightly, eyeing the food on the platter.

Then he looked up at her. 'It is useless, *chérie*. I cannot eat until you tell me these mysterious things.'

'Neither can I,' said Portia in relief, and jumped up. 'Let's go into the other room, then.' She curled up in a corner of the sofa, and patted the cushion beside her in invitation. Heat leapt in Luc's eyes for a moment, but he sat down gingerly, very careful not to touch her. 'How is your mother?' she asked.

'Since your visit she is much changed,' he said soberly. 'Now she has faced the truth about Olivier at last she no longer wishes to live at Beau Rivage. Her plan is to make a new home for herself, somewhere near Ghislaine or Amélie, and expend her care and energies on her remaining family, instead of the son who died.'

'I'm glad. Now I've had time to recover I can feel sympathy for her. And for poor young Olly.'

'Portia, it is you I am concerned with at this moment, not my mother, nor Olivier.' Luc turned towards her and took her hand. 'Am I right in assuming you remember what happened that September?'

She nodded. 'The moment I saw those photographs in your attic it all came rushing back. Although in some ways it began before then. From the day I met you, I suppose. I couldn't understand why your voice, your accent, was so familiar. I knew I'd never seen you before, yet in the beginning I felt so wary, as though you spelt danger for me in some way.'

'Do you still feel like that?'

'No. Because I know now that your voice reminded me of your brother. I found it tantalisingly familiar, but I couldn't remember where I'd heard it before.' She leaned against him, and Luc tensed, then put his arm round her, waiting, Portia knew, to see if she would push him away. When she merely settled herself comfortably in the crook of his arm he let out a deep breath, then drew her close as she began, hesitantly at first, to tell the unpleasant story of her lost September.

When she'd finished Luc sat very still for a moment, his face set in grim lines. Then he lifted her onto his lap and cradled her against his shoulder. 'And I am to blame for bringing that back to you,' he said bitterly.

Portia raised her face to his, her eyes shining. 'But I'm glad, Luc. All those years I was sure I was responsible for Mr Radford's death. I felt like a murderer. I knew he was alive when he went to the hospital, but I couldn't remember what happened before I was found in the hall with him.'

'*Mon Dieu*, it is no wonder you feared a return to Turret House!'

'I tried to make myself go back several times, convinced I had only to cross the threshold and it would all come rushing back. But I couldn't bring myself to do it, terrified of what I'd find out. And in the end it didn't work, anyway. I dreaded setting foot inside the tower most of all, but when I did, even the turret room was just an empty space. I felt something,' she added, 'when I saw the new Aga. But not enough to remind me of what I'd done with the old one.'

Luc's eyes locked with hers. 'Tell me, Portia. Was this gap in your memory the reason why you refused to marry me?'

'Of course it was. But I couldn't stop myself falling in love with you. Or staying in love,' she added huskily, her eyes falling.

Luc let out a long, unsteady breath, then kissed her with such tenderness tears leaked from the corners of Portia's eyes. 'Do not cry, *mon amour*,' he said against her lips.

'I'm crying because I'm happy,' she whispered, and said nothing else for a long time as Luc kissed her with a mounting passion she responded to with a rush of desire fuelled by the relief of telling Luc her secret. When she felt Luc draw away she opened her eyes in protest, to find his eyes glittering with determination in his set face.

'First there are confessions to make, Portia—'

'No, please, you don't have to,' she interrupted.

'Yes, *mignonne*, I do,' he said heavily. 'In future there must be no shadows between us.'

She reached a hand to his cheek, then put her head on his shoulder. 'All right, Luc. Though nothing will make any difference to the way I feel about you—'

Luc's mouth came down on hers to cut off her words as he kissed her with passionate thanksgiving. Then he smoothed her head down against his shoulder again, silent for a moment as he searched for words to explain. 'First, Portia,' he began, 'you must understand how it was with my mother and Olivier. She idolised him. All his life she gave him everything he wanted the moment he asked, first toys, then later boats and cars. So when he wanted you, *chérie*, he made my mother pay someone to search for you. When this failed, he grew wild, began drinking heavily.'

Portia took his hand and held it tightly.

'Olivier,' continued Luc harshly, 'drove too fast always, believing himself immortal, as boys of his age always do. One night his luck deserted him when he took a corner too fast on his way home from a party. No one else was hurt, *Dieu merci*. But my mother was mad with grief, and perhaps guilt also, because it was she who bought him the powerful car he was driving. She needed someone to blame—'

'So she chose me,' said Portia quietly.

Luc nodded. 'She persuaded herself that Olivier killed himself because of you. It became an obsession with her. I became truly afraid for her reason. My sisters, also. When I bought the Hampstead flat from Whitefriars and found you worked for the agency it seemed like fate. So I decided to end this nonsense of my mother's. Your Mr Parrish had given me details of Turret House, giving me the perfect way to meet you, but I had not expected to fall so desperately in love, *mignonne*,' he added huskily, and Portia drew his head down to hers, kissing him passionately to show she felt the same.

'At first,' he said unevenly, when he could bring himself to continue, 'I merely intended to ask if you'd been in love with Olivier. But once I met you I was more concerned with making you love *me*. When my mother heard I'd found you,' he went on heavily, 'she insisted I take you to Beau Rivage. I planned to tell you everything that weekend, certain that when my mother met you she would know at once that you had nothing to do with Olivier's death.'

Portia shivered. 'Instead your mother said I virtually killed him. She told me her plan was for you to seduce me, then abandon me, to inflict the pain Olivier suffered.'

Luc's mouth twisted in distaste as he pulled her closer. 'Portia, I did not agree to this, I swear. Can you believe that?' He brought her face up to his, his face relaxing slightly as she smiled up into his eyes.

'Of course I do. Now. But that horrible day I was trying to cope with far too many things at once. My missing memory would have been enough on its own, but when your mother implied you were a willing ac-

complice to her revenge I was so shattered I just got in
the car and took off for St Malo.'

'My mother sent me off on a fool's errand, with some
story of an accident to Ghislaine,' said Luc bitterly.
'When my sister confessed Maman had told her to keep
me there I broke the speed limit back to Beau Rivage.
Then I arrived to find you gone and learned my mother
had disobeyed me. I was so enraged with her that she
was frightened into facing reality at last.'

'Luc, don't blame her too much,' said Portia quickly.
'If she hadn't taken me up to the attic I might still be
in the dark about the gap in my memory. In which case,'
she added, 'there would have been no hope of—of anything permanent between us.'

Luc smiled, looking suddenly younger, as though a
great weight had rolled from his shoulders. 'Why can
you not say marriage?'

She flushed, her eyes falling from the look in his. 'It
seemed to be taking too much for granted,' she muttered,
and he laughed outright, and bent his head to kiss her.
But after a moment he put her away, breathing hard. 'I
cannot kiss you like this without wanting so much more.
And I am determined to show you that it is not just your
beautiful body I desire. I want all of you, Portia.'

'I want all of you, too.' She smiled at him with such
undisguised love in her eyes Luc crushed her to him.

'These past weeks have been a torment,' he muttered
into her hair.

'For me too,' she assured him, and pushed at his re-
straining hands.

He dropped them at once and Portia got to her feet,
her hands going to the pins securing her hair. Luc
watched as she took them out, one by one, then she

shook her hair free and smiled at him, and he leapt to his feet and swept her up into his arms.

'Until you did that I thought I could exist without making love to you, but it is impossible—'

'I thought it might be,' she admitted, then blushed vividly as Luc threw back his head and laughed joyously, and she laughed with him.

They were still laughing when they fell on her bed together, undressing each other with caressing, unsteady hands. But when she was naked in his arms Luc's laughter died, and he laid his face between her breasts, his breath hot against her skin.

'I persuaded myself I would not expect this,' he said indistinctly.

Portia balanced on an elbow and ran her free hand through his thick dark hair. 'This morning, when I rang your office and found you were away, I was sure this would never happen again.'

Luc smiled up at her in triumph. 'I was on my way here to find you. We were meant to be together, Portia. Fate led me to find you that day. And I am keeping you.'

He began to caress her, his hands cool and his mouth hot as they enticed her into a response made all the fiercer by their separation. As she began caresses of her own Luc stiffened and muttered something French and indistinct in her ear.

'Yes, please,' she said breathlessly. 'I'd like that.'

Luc raised his head to stare down into her glittering eyes. 'You understood?'

She smiled exultantly. 'I've been studying in secret.'

He held her arms wide, keeping her pinned beneath him. 'Is there anything else you should confess?' he demanded.

She nodded, and he waited, poised tense above her.

'Tell me, Portia!'

'It's just something I've been practising in secret.' She took in a deep breath, her eyes holding his. '*Je t'aime beaucoup*, Luc.'

He let out an unsteady breath and released her hands to bury his face in her hair for a moment, then he kissed her with an urgency he could no longer control, her response so explicit he lifted her hips and took possession of her, their need for each other so overwhelming they were swiftly consumed by the fierce heat of their reunion.

They stayed locked in each other's arms for a long time afterwards, luxuriating in the bliss of reconciliation. But at last Portia struggled free.

'What is it, *mignonne*?' demanded Luc.

'I'm hungry!'

On a beautiful early summer day a few weeks later Portia walked down the church aisle, smiling up at the man beside her. The smile stayed through all the kissing and hugging, and the photographic session outside the church, but once the photographer pronounced himself satisfied Portia found herself firmly detached from the wedding group.

'Who is that man you were clinging to?' demanded Luc.

'Hal's friend. And I wasn't clinging. The chief bridesmaid always walks arm in arm with the best man,' said Portia happily. 'Besides, you know perfectly well you're the best man where I'm concerned.' She gave him an approving head-to-toe look. 'You look wonderful.'

'I like your dress, also,' said Luc, eyeing her narrow sheath of midnight-blue silk. 'Very elegant, *ma belle*. However,' he added conversationally, 'I would like very much to tear it off you right now. It is two endless weeks since we were together.'

'What on earth are you saying, Luc Brissac?' called Marianne. 'It's the bride who's supposed to blush, not the bridesmaid.'

The reception at the Taylors' home was a happy, informal affair, where most of the guests mingled at will. But Luc flatly refused to move from Portia's side the entire time, to the amusement of all concerned.

'Can't say I blame you,' said the bride's father, patting Portia's cheek. 'You're a lucky man, Luc,' he added, and beckoned a waiter to refill their glasses.

'I know this,' Luc assured him.

Mr Taylor winked, then went off to see to the rest of his guests. Soon it was time for speeches, and toasts to the bridesmaids, then the cake was cut, and at last Marianne went off with her mother to change.

'Soon,' said Luc, 'we shall be able to go, *n'est ce pas*?'

'Yes,' said Portia, and smiled up at him. 'What do you think of a traditional British wedding?'

'Most charming. But very long. I have made so much conversation my English is beginning to desert me.'

'Like it does in bed,' she whispered, and his eyes darkened.

'It no longer matters, since you now understand everything I say.'

She smiled demurely. 'Not quite everything.'

'Tonight I shall translate every word,' he promised, sliding an arm round her.

'Luc, can you let Portia go for a minute?' called Hal. 'Marianne wants her.'

'Not as much as I do,' muttered Luc, but he released

his hold on Portia's waist and watched her go upstairs before joining Hal and his best man.

Marianne was waiting in her room, ready for her honeymoon in the suit they'd chosen together. 'Well, then, Portia. It's done. The knot's tied.'

'Are you happy?' said Portia.

'Very. Luc looks happy too. I take it things are settled?'

Portia nodded. 'Beau Rivage is reverting to a hotel again. Madame Brissac has found a house near Ghislaine and her family, and Luc and I are going to alternate between his apartment in Paris and the one he's bought in London.'

'So it's happy-ever-after time for us both,' said Marianne with satisfaction.

'I never really thought it would be for me,' said Portia soberly, and they hugged each other convulsively, until a knock on the door broke them apart.

'Come *on*, Mrs Courtney, or we'll miss our flight,' yelled Hal. 'There's another impatient guy out here too. Luc wants his wife back.'

The two friends looked at each other, blinked a little, then smiled and went to join the men waiting for them outside on the landing.

'I hope you haven't been putting my bridegroom off the joys of wedded bliss,' said Marianne, laughing up at Luc.

'*Au contraire*, Madame Courtney.' Luc grinned wickedly. 'I am as eager to resume my marriage as Hal is to begin his.'

'I'm surprised you let Portia work out her notice alone in London,' said Marianne, as the four of them went downstairs together.

'It was the only way I could get her to marry me so

quickly,' he said with regret. 'It is no way to conduct a marriage, with the bridegroom in Provence and the bride in London.'

'We had a honeymoon at that gorgeous château first,' pointed out his wife.

'True. But it was not long enough.'

Later, after Luc and Portia had waved off the bridal pair and taken protracted leave of their hosts, Luc got into the car with a sigh of relief. 'A mile or two only, *chérie*, and we can be alone at last.'

Portia gave him a startled look. 'I thought we were going back to London tonight.'

'No, we are not.' Luc smiled smugly as they drove away from the Taylor home. 'I booked a room at a very pleasing little country hotel not far from here, *mignonne*.'

Portia began to laugh. 'You are a very high-handed man, Luc Brissac.'

'Do you mind that I am so eager to be alone with you?'

'No. Not a bit. It's a brilliant idea. I can't think why I didn't think of it myself.'

'Because you are a woman, *chérie*.'

'What's that got to do with it?'

'A man who exists without his very new wife for two long weeks is naturally obsessed with thoughts of taking her to bed the moment he sees her again. With a woman it is sadly different.'

'Not this woman,' said Portia, and gave him a wicked little smile. 'Your wife is in complete accord, Monsieur Brissac. Can't you drive a bit faster?'

HARLEQUIN® *Presents*

Set in the steamy Australian outback
a fabulous new triology by
bestselling Presents author

Emma Darcy

Kings of the
Outback

Three masterful brothers
and the women who tame them

On sale June
THE CATTLE KING'S MISTRESS
Harlequin Presents®, #2110

On sale July
THE PLAYBOY KING'S WIFE
Harlequin Presents®, #2116

On sale August
THE PLEASURE KING'S BRIDE
Harlequin Presents®, #2122

Available wherever Harlequin books are sold.

HARLEQUIN®
Makes any time special ™

Visit us at www.eHarlequin.com   HPKING

If you enjoyed what you just read,
then we've got an offer you can't resist!

Take 2 bestselling
love stories FREE!
Plus get a FREE surprise gift!

Clip this page and mail it to Harlequin Reader Service®

IN U.S.A.	IN CANADA
3010 Walden Ave.	P.O. Box 609
P.O. Box 1867	Fort Erie, Ontario
Buffalo, N.Y. 14240-1867	L2A 5X3

YES! Please send me 2 free Harlequin Presents® novels and my free surprise gift. Then send me 6 brand-new novels every month, which I will receive months before they're available in stores. In the U.S.A., bill me at the bargain price of $3.34 plus 25¢ delivery per book and applicable sales tax, if any*. In Canada, bill me at the bargain price of $3.74 plus 25¢ delivery per book and applicable taxes**. That's the complete price and a savings of at least 10% off the cover prices—what a great deal! I understand that accepting the 2 free books and gift places me under no obligation ever to buy any books. I can always return a shipment and cancel at any time. Even if I never buy another book from Harlequin, the 2 free books and gift are mine to keep forever. So why not take us up on our invitation. You'll be glad you did!

106 HEN C22Q
306 HEN C22R

Name	(PLEASE PRINT)	
Address	Apt.#	
City	State/Prov.	Zip/Postal Code

* Terms and prices subject to change without notice. Sales tax applicable in N.Y.
** Canadian residents will be charged applicable provincial taxes and GST.
  All orders subject to approval. Offer limited to one per household.
  ® are registered trademarks of Harlequin Enterprises Limited.

PRES00   ©1998 Harlequin Enterprises Limited

Coming in June from

HARLEQUIN

AMERICAN ◆ ROMANCE®

MAITLAND MATERNITY

When two sets
of twins are born at
Maitland Maternity Hospital on
the same day, unforgettable surprises
are sure to follow. Don't miss the fun, the
romance, the joy...as two special couples find
love just outside the delivery room door.

Watch for:
SURPRISE! SURPRISE!
by Tina Leonard
On sale June█████.

I DO! I DO!
by Jacqueline Diamond
On sale July█████

And there will be many more Maitland Maternity
stories when a special twelve-book continuity series
launches in Augus█████
Don't miss any of these stories by wonderful
authors such as Marie Ferrarella, Jule McBride,
Muriel Jensen and Judy Christenberry.

Available at your favorite retail outlet.

HARLEQUIN®
Makes any time special ™

Visit us at www.eHarlequin.com.

HARMMDD

makes any time special—online...

your romantic
life

➤ Talk to Dr. Romance, find a romantic recipe, or send a
virtual hint to the love of your life. You'll find great
articles and advice on romantic issues that are close to
your heart.

your romantic
books

➤ Visit our *Author's Alcove* and try your hand in the Writing
Round Robin—contribute a chapter to an online book in
the making.

➤ Enter the *Reading Room* for an interactive novel—help
determine the fate of a story being created now by one
of your favorite authors.

➤ Drop into *Books & More!* for the latest releases—read
an excerpt, find this month's Harlequin
top sellers.

your romantic
escapes

➤ Escape into romantic movies at *Reel Love*,
learn what the stars have in store for you
with *Lovescopes*, treat yourself to our
Indulgences Guides and get away to the
latest romantic hot spots in *Romantic Travel*.

All this and more available at
www.eHarlequin.com
on Women.com Networks

HECHAN1

Back by popular demand are
DEBBIE MACOMBER's

Hard Luck, Alaska, is a town that needs women! And the O'Halloran brothers are just the fellows to fly them in.

Starting in March ██████ this beloved series returns in special 2-in-1 collector's editions:

MAIL-ORDER MARRIAGES, featuring
Brides for Brothers and *The Marriage Risk*
On sale March ██

FAMILY MEN, featuring
Daddy's Little Helper and *Because of the Baby*
On sale July ████

THE LAST TWO BACHELORS, featuring
Falling for Him and *Ending in Marriage*
On sale August ████

Collect and enjoy each MIDNIGHT SONS story!

Available at your favorite retail outlet.

HARLEQUIN®
Makes any time special ™

Visit us at www.romance.net

PHMS